Clash of the Titans - The Wentworth Pack 05

The Wentworth Pack 1 Jory's Destiny, Volume 5

Haley Langwood

Published by Haley Langwood, 2024.

CLASH OF THE TITANS - THE WENTWORTH PACK 05

First edition. July 11, 2024.

Copyright © 2024 Haley Langwood.

ISBN: 979-8227167972

Written by Haley Langwood.

Table of Contents

Chapter One

About six months ago, they battled Dhidysus, Leldur, and Zachariah. Then, out of the blue, the three had disappeared, and ever since, it had been peaceful, like they had never existed. However, Eric and Jory knew that even though everything looked fine, it wasn't. They knew that it was the proverbial silence before the storm.

In that same period, Eric had stepped down, and Rose had taken over managing the ranch. She graduated cum laude and now had her master's degree in economics and business. Plus, Rose loved horses, their well-being came first, and that's why she was so successful. Now she was blessed with a mate, and a beautiful little girl, Caitlin.

It had been quiet and peaceful for the last couple of months, with no attacks and no threats, and Eric and Jory enjoyed every moment. They often had taken the children to the pond because one of Christopher's spirits was a dolphin. So, the boy could shift at the pond and have fun in the water. Jory could watch his son for hours while frolicking in the pond, throwing frisbees and beach balls at Jory, who threw them back at him. His dolphin was a magnificent white animal.

Other than the dolphin, Christopher shared his soul with a white wolf, white lion, white poodle, and hawk. The hawk was the only one who had his natural color. Why? That was anyone's guess. Every now and then, the boy was allowed to fly above the QH Ranch. Eric and Jory didn't like it but knew that the hawk, like Christopher's other spirits, needed to fly on occasion. If not, the animal would go mad, which was dangerous for the boy. It was a danger for any shifter if they couldn't let their counterparts run or fly regularly.

Carmen was a serious child; she always carried at least one book with her. She mostly sat beside Eric while reading. Carmen still was hesitant to let her wolf out more often. Eric and Jory had tried to talk to Carmen about her wolf, but the girl turned and walked away whenever they brought up the issue. So, the alpha and his mate had stopped asking her, hoping she would one day open up to them.

They often took the kids horseback riding, which Christopher also enjoyed because when with his daddies, they headed for the forest. If he went horseback riding alone, he wasn't permitted to leave the property because it was too dangerous. Eric and Jory knew that their little boy was very powerful, but he still was just a little boy who should have fun, not fight monsters.

Eric and Jory sat on the back deck, enjoying the weather while watching their children. Christopher was riding Beau, and Carmen sat on the swing, reading a book. Even though Jory looked relaxed, he wasn't because his gut feeling told him something was about to happen. "Is something wrong, baby?" Eric quietly asked his mate. Jory shook his head. "I'm not sure, but something definitely feels off," he softly replied. He was proven right when Carmen jumped off the swing and rushed toward them. Christopher joined them a few minutes later, looking expectantly at his sister.

Jory looked from Christopher to Carmen, who stood before them, staring from him to Eric. "Is there something we should know?" the alpha mate carefully questioned. The children eyed each other, and Jory knew they were using their unique mind link to communicate.

It was Carmen who finally spoke. "Aunt Gaia wants to talk to you. She will summon us soon." Eric and Jory eyed each other, and Jory knew he should be surprised, but he wasn't. Somehow, he had known that this day was coming.

Jory called JJ to ask him to take care of Beau, Christopher's horse. The moment Carmen jumped off the swing, Christopher dismounted his horse and ran toward his fathers. Now the boy wanted to return to the small meadow where Beau was patiently waiting. However, Jory and Eric didn't want to let the boy out of their side. Armand would orb JJ to safety if necessary, but Jordan could hold his own since he was half shifter and half vampire.

"Dad, I want to take the dogs for a walk," Carmen said. "I'd rather you stay here on the back deck," Jory replied as he gently stroked her cheek. "I'm not in danger, dad. Aunt Gaia won't harm me," Carmen looked expectantly at Jory. Jory eyed Eric, silently asking for his opinion. The alpha smiled, watched his mate, and said, "I think Carmen can take the dogs for a walk safely. Gaia would never harm her or Christopher."

"I'll stay in the garden, promise," Carmen smiled as she went inside to get the four dogs. A while ago, Jory had put Digger to sleep because the old dog was in pain, and that would only worsen. Then, Christopher brought home a stray dog who was in labor. So now they had Dudley, Molly, and her two pups, Sage and Chloe.

Eric cocked his head, listening. "James and Max are here," the alpha said as he stood, pulling a frowning Jory with him. "Did we forget they were coming?" the alpha mate questioned. "No, we didn't," Eric replied.

James opened the car's back door and freed Marcus from his seatbelt. The boy immediately jumped out of the vehicle and ran inside the house. "I assume that Christopher is in the garden?" Max smiled, but it didn't reach her beautiful baby blue eyes. James took Grace from the car seat, and then they walked inside the house.

"Not that I'm not happy to see you, but what brings you here? You look worried," Jory began as they walked toward the front door.

Max sighed as she eyed her mate. "Marcus told us to come to the ranch," she looked at James, then added, "He didn't tell us why, though." They walked inside, straight into the garden, where the boys played with the dogs. James put Grace on the ground, and the girl immediately ran toward Carmen, who had just returned from the back of the garden with four dogs in tow. The girls took a seat on the swing, and it seemed as if Carmen was explaining her book to Grace.

Eric went inside to get drinks for everyone; he was followed by James. Max looked worried, and Jory knew she had reason to be concerned. She eyed her friend. "Do you know what this is all about?"

"I do, but let's wait for Eric and James to return," the alpha mate quietly replied.

"Is this for real?" Max whispered. "Yes, Aunt Max. It's very real," Christopher answered before Eric or Jory could. "When," James asked. "I'm not sure, but soon. Maybe tomorrow, maybe the day after that," the boy replied. Eric, Jory, Max, and James were stunned when their children continued enjoying their snacks as if nothing had happened. "Our kids act like everything is alright. They don't seem afraid; I don't understand, and it scares the hell out of me," Max whispered.

Jory knew that Max wasn't afraid for herself but for the safety of their children. "So, let me summarize," said James. Eric and Jory nodded, and when no one replied, the sheriff continued. "So, Gaia, or Mother Earth, wants to talk to us? Will she come here?" "I don't think that it's that simple. My gut feeling tells me that something big is about to happen. And it will involve our children," Jory explained. The alpha mate knew that all four of the children would be involved. He didn't like it, and neither did James, Max, and Eric.

"If Gaia doesn't show up today, then I want you to stay at the ranch," the alpha said. "I'm curious about her plans for the children. I hate to be kept in the dark when it concerns the kid's safety," the white tiger softly growled. Jory nodded because he felt the same. However, the alpha mate also knew whatever Gaia's plans were; there was nothing they could do. "We just have to wait and see what it is that she wants," said Jory. As if on cue, everything quieted down. However, Beau and the four dogs seemed relaxed, which was good. Max looked around and was surprised because she felt no panic, just serenity.

Then mist slowly enveloped them. Carmen held Eric's hand and Christopher Jory's. Marcus and Grace did the same with their parents. Suddenly the fog receded, and a beautiful garden became visible. Max was in awe, making Jory chuckle. "I've been here before," he clarified after seeing Max's expression. "Oh. Okay," was all Max could muster.

James, who was holding his mate and children tightly, looked around; his expression was unreadable. "It's alright, James. Gaia would never hurt the children. Don't forget; they are related," Jory spoke calmly, not wanting to spook James or Max. Eric seemed calm, and Jory knew that it was because of him. The alpha trusted his mate completely.

Chapter Two

They felt her presence before they saw her. Max gasped as Gaia appeared in front of them. She smiled warmly at Jory, and then a second woman appeared beside her. Gaia turned her head slightly sideways. "About time," she chuckled.

"You were gone so fast; I didn't have time to close the shop," the woman replied. "Meet Destiny," Gaia said. Destiny eyed Max and James intently; then, she looked at Marcus and Grace Madison. "I did well, didn't I?" she addressed Gaia. "You did, indeed," Mother Earth gently smiled.

Gaia eyed the children, her expression gentle. "Come and let me hug you," she said in a near whisper. The four children didn't hesitate as they ran into Mother Earth's waiting arms. After hugging them, Gaia held the kids at arm's length; she said in a kind voice, "You are perfect, so beautiful and brave." It looked as if Destiny wanted to say something; she opened her mouth but closed it again.

Jory wanted to know why they were summoned, but his instinct told him to keep his mouth shut. "Be patient, my child; I will explain why you are here shortly," Gaia softly said. Mother Earth first looked at Jory; then, she eyed Eric, Max, and James. Max and James were mesmerized by Gaia's beauty, but they couldn't tell what she looked like. Then again, no one really could, not even Jory or the children.

"What I am about to ask of you will be the ultimate sacrifice all of you will need to make. As it concerns your children," Gaia spoke in a soft voice, but they had heard her perfectly. When no one said anything, she continued. "About six months ago, Destiny and I managed to capture Dhidysus, Leldur, and Zachariah. However, to keep them restrained, we needed Chaos. We didn't like it, but it wasn't like we had a choice. Somehow Dhidysus and Leldur gained very much power; we're still looking into that because we want to know who provided them with extra power," Gaia paused and looked at Destiny.

"Who is Chaos?" Jory quietly questioned. He probably was the only one who was allowed to ask questions. Gaia, even though gentle and kind, didn't tolerate interruption. You only spoke to her when she addressed you directly. However, Jory, somehow, had pulled it off to befriend Gaia, well, sort off. After all, she was Mother Earth.

Gaia looked at Destiny again and nodded for her to explain about Chaos. "Chaos is *the* God, the first of us; he was the one who filled the gap between Heaven and Earth. He created the first beings known to us as Gaia," she pointed at Mother Earth. Then she went on. "Tartarus, Nyx, Erebos, and Uranus. Although no one knows how he came into existence, you could say that Chaos is the nothingness that all else sprung from." Destiny paused for a short moment, then she said matter of factly, "Some say that he's even older than earth. That he was the one who created the earth." Eric, James, and Max looked confused, but Jory understood. He said, "It's like Chaos caused the big bang that created Earth?" Destiny smiled approvingly, and was that pride in Gaia's eyes?

Before Destiny spoke again, Carmen went to sit beside Eric, and Christopher took his place beside Jory. Marcus and Grace did the same; the boy sat beside Max and the girl beside her father.

Destiny gently smiled at the children; then, her expression turned serious. "As Gaia said earlier, we will ask you to make the biggest sacrifice of your life. As you know, Dhidysus and Leldur gained more power. However, the one to watch out for is Zachariah because the one who provided Dhidysus and Leldur with extra power did the same with Zachariah."

"This is bad because they will eventually come after Christopher again, right?" a horrified Jory whispered. It was Gaia who answered the alpha mate. "I'm afraid so, my child." "We won't let that happen," Eric growled. Gaia eyed the alpha, and Eric couldn't tell if she was offended that he had spoken or that she approved his interruption.

"You are correct, we won't let that happen, but the problem is, only the children can fight Zachariah and prevail. But, for that to happen, they need to grow up fast. We can make that happen. But, even though the children are our creation, we need you the consent of what we are about to do," Destiny said, looking at the children.

Gaia eyed Eric as if reading his mind; she said, "Even a powerful creature such as yourself isn't powerful enough to beat Dhidysus, Leldur, and Zachariah. So if you fight them, it will mean your demise." Eric frowned, and Jory looked horrified.

It was James who spoke. "How can that be? Eric is one of the most powerful beings we know." "I'm confused because our children are far too young to fight against Gods and, well, whatever Zachariah is." Max, who had both of her children tightly in her arms, said. She looked at James and added, "We can't allow our children to battle; they are only babies."

"Please, hear me out before you draw conclusions," Gaia said. Then, when she had everyone's attention, children included, Gaia began to explain.

******

They sat on the back deck, staring at each other. "I still can't believe what she suggested. And what it has to do with Marcus and Grace," Max said. Jory sighed because he knew their kids were special after all; they were the children created by Gaia and some of the Gods. This was what he had been afraid of from the moment they found Christopher and then Carmen.

Jory had always known that Christopher and Carmen had been sent to them for a reason. However, Gaia's explanation had shocked the hell out of him, and not only him, Eric, and James were furious, and Max was horrified.

"I don't like it," Max said. "I agree, but we need to talk to the children, see how they feel about it," Jory replied. "I know, but, damn, they are so young." "They are, but you know as well as I do that they are special," Jory said. Max nodded because she knew Jory was right, but her maternal instinct told her to protect her children at all costs.

Max eyed Jory. "I don't know if James and I give our consent for Gaia to proceed. For God's sake, Jory, they are children, small children; how can we ask them what they want, how they feel?" the white tiger shifter whispered, sounding desperate.

Before Jory could tell his best friend how he and Eric thought about it, the four children came to stand in front of them. Marcus took his mother's hand; looking straight into her eyes, he said, "Mom, it's okay. Grace and I want to do this. We need to do this."

Max's eyes filled with tears as she eyed her precious son. "Sweetheart, how can you say that? I know that you and Grace are special, but you're too young to understand what it is that you will face." Then, she looked at Christopher and Carmen and finally at Grace and Marcus. "Do you realize that you lose at least twenty years?"

"No, we won't. Aunt Gaia explained it to us. We will have memories of those, what you call lost years. Mom, please? Grace and I really want to do this," Marcus said in a soft but determined tone. "It's true, Aunt Max. We all want to do this. No, we need to do this because if we don't, then we will never be safe. We can't grow up looking over our shoulders every single day," Christopher chimed in.

Jory and Eric frowned because it seemed that the children had already decided that they would go with Gaia's plan. Christopher and Carmen eyed Eric and Jory, and no words were needed by the look on the children's faces. Jory looked at Max; he softly said, "I don't like it any more than you do, but it looks like the children made their choice."

The white tiger looked at her mate. "I don't know. What do you think, James," Max asked tentatively. The sheriff sighed, and Jory knew what he was about to say and that it would break Max's heart. Max had seen it, too, because her eyes showed devastation. "No, James, not you too." "Max, sweetheart. I trust our children, and if they say they want to do this, then who are we to stop them?"

When Max opened her mouth to protest, he held up his hand, gently silencing her. "Yes, I agree with Marcus and Grace, and no, I don't like it one bit because I want them safe." James cupped Max's face as he gently kissed her and softly said. "Sweetheart, I'm afraid we don't have a choice."

Jory looked at Eric because the alpha was the only one who hadn't shared his thoughts. Eric pressed his lips together before he finally spoke. "If it were up to me, I would take on Zachariah, Dhidysus, and Leldur. But, apparently, it takes Christopher, Carmen, Marcus, and Grace to take those three down, once and for all."

Chapter Three

It was morning, and Jory's heart broke at seeing a devastated Max. Even though they all had problems with consenting to Gaia's plan, the white tiger was very upset. It had hit Max and James hard. The Stantons hadn't known that their children had been created by the Gods as well, just like Christopher and Carmen.

The knowledge had come as a shock, and now the four kids had to battle two Gods and, well, Jory's Uncle Zachariah. Zachariah was the brother of the Archangel Dacian, who created Finn, Jory's father. Zachariah had turned into a mighty warlock when he joined the dark side; ever since, no one had been able to kill him simply because he was protected by pitch dark magic.

The warlock had been after Christopher from the moment Eric and Jory had adopted the boy. He had known from the beginning just how unique and powerful the child was, and he wanted that power. So, Eric and Jory knew how dangerous Zachariah was, and this monster had the help of two Gods. What a fucking mess.

Jory could tell Max had been crying, and he understood perfectly why. The alpha mate was worried because he had no idea what impact the whole ordeal would have on them. He had never even heard of aging someone in record time.

"When will you let Gaia know about our decision?" Max questioned, looking from Jory to Eric. "Soon, after I've gone through everything one more time. So, probably around noon," Jory sighed and added in a whisper, "It's no use postponing the inevitable." "I guess not," Max softly said. Marcus and Grace hugged their mother tightly, comforting her as best as possible.

Gaia had explained that to battle Leldur, Dhidysus, and of course Zachariah and prevail, the children needed to age, fast. Mother Earth had explained that with the help of Chaos and Destiny, she would be able to age the children twenty years. However, she had warned them that the entire process would take about a month, maybe even longer.

"Are you alright?" Eric questioned as he sat down next to his mate. They sat on the bench in the garden, under the old oak. Jory let his head rest against Eric's chest. "She wants to age them twenty years in a month. It's hard to comprehend that our precious children get their personal, fake memories. Imagine twenty years of memories from which we know they're not real." Before the alpha mate could say more, bright lights appeared, and a moment later, Destiny stood in front of them.

"I'm sorry for eavesdropping on your conversation, but I sensed fear, uncertainty, and anger," she had a pleasant voice, soft, gentle. It was a voice that soothed if you liked it or not. Jory instantly calmed. As if on cue, James and Max appeared in the garden and sat down on the other bench. Destiny nodded at the sheriff and the white tiger. Then, she turned her head and eyed Jory; Destiny knew that the alpha mate was about to speak.

"Forgive me for asking, but it really is hard to fathom that the children will be fed with memories that are not theirs. Just like that, you are about to take twenty years away from them, twenty years. Yes, I know it's necessary, but they are our children, and we want the best for them. I'm still not convinced that aging them and sending them into a war is in their best interest. As a father, I have my doubts, as you surely will understand," the alpha mate said.

"And Eric and Jory are not the only ones. James and I have doubts as well. I'm still horrified at the thought of what you're planning to do with the children. What impact will it have on their future? Will they be able to accept everything that you will put them through and live a happy life without mental problems?" Max asked.

Destiny nodded in understanding; she looked serious when she spoke, "As you know, I'm Destiny, and that's why I know what the future will bring for the whole pack, including you, James, Max, and your children. So, the memories we will feed them are real. Everything they would have experienced in those twenty years will be their memories, and we will do the same with you. All the memories we will put into your mind will be the real deal."

"I'm sorry, but you lost me," Max said when a bright light caught their attention and a second later, Gaia appeared, and she wasn't alone. Next to her stood a very handsome man, his strawberry blond hair reaching his waist. He had eyes as dark as night, and there was something magical surrounding him. Jory was mesmerized by the man's appearance, but he wasn't the only one; Eric, James, and Max were as well.

Gaia chuckled as she introduced Chaos. So, this was the one that created the earth. Chaos kept his distance as he stared from one to the other. Gaia watched Chaos for a while before she addressed Jory, Eric, James, and Max.

"Chaos never interfered with humans before. So, that he's here shows how dire the situation is," said Gaia. Chaos didn't speak, but he was observing everyone and everything. "What Destiny said is correct," Gaia continued, "She's able to see the future of all of you, and I can assure you that the children won't get one memory that's not theirs."

"But we will miss so much, like seeing them grow up, their first love," Max whispered. Gaia shook her head and explained patiently again that they, as parents, would get their memories of their children growing up and reaching adulthood. But what was even more important, Gaia assured her once again that all memories were real.

Suddenly Max looked up, eyes wide, as she looked at her wristwatch. "Where are the children?" she cried out. "Annabella and Felicia are watching them. Right now, they are playing with the dogs on the blanket next to the fireplace," Destiny said, smiling gently. This seemed to ease Max's mind enough to make her a bit more relaxed.

"What will happen when their aging is completed? How will you go from there." It was Eric who had spoken; the alpha hadn't said anything until now.

"They will be ready to attack and defend their home, family, and friends. Plus, Chaos, Ares, and The Fates, known as Clotho, Lachesis, and Atropos, will be on standby should their help become necessary. But, whatever happens, we will do everything in our power to keep the children alive," Gaia informed them, her voice soothing as she gently smiled down at them.

"Who are The Fates?" Jory questioned. Gaia's expression was unreadable when she answered. "They are three mysterious sisters, and when I say mysterious, I mean mysterious. Even I have never seen them. I know they exist, though. They have offered their help because it's what they are supposed to do. At least, that's how it was explained to me. The three of them affect the paths of everyone in the universe." Gaia paused while eying the children, who were solely focused on her.

It takes a moment but finally, she continues. "There is Clotho; it's her who spins the thread of life. Then we have Lachesis, she is the one who assigns each person's thread, and finally, Atropos, we need to watch for her because she cuts the thread of life at its end, which means that she ends your life. So, there's a lot you need to know, but we will feed you all the necessary information while you sleep and receive the memories of you and your children while they grow up."

Max looked up at Gaia, but it was James who spoke. "Forgive me for asking this, but I can't comprehend how you want to let the children grow and provide them with memories that didn't take place."

Gaia looked at Destiny and nodded. Destiny looked thoughtful for a moment, searching for the right word to explain so that Eric, Jory, James, and Max understood.

"Alright, to let the children grow physically is easy. However, to provide them with their personal memories, well, that's a bit more complicated. It's best if you picture numerous small pieces floating around each child. They float and wait until it's time for them to become a memory. Then, as soon as one of those memories happens, it will flow into the child's mind and becomes a memory. It's up to me to see to it that there are no complications. So, this part of aging will take most of the time. It's why I need at least a month, maybe even more. Then there's the four of you who will get the same treatment," Destiny eyed James in question. "Thank you for explaining, so we all understand," James said.

"It could even take more than a month because I will take my time to make it happen and keep your sanity intact," Destiny softly added. It was quiet after that, it took a long time, and it was Max who finally spoke.

The white tiger sounded broken. "This is the hardest decision we've ever made, and I really don't want to do this, but James and I know that we don't actually have a choice. Marcus and Grace already let us know that they think it's meant to be because it's their destiny," Max said in a barely audible voice. It was obvious that she was in agony.

Jory wanted to comfort her, assuring his friend that it would be alright, but he didn't know if it would be okay. The last thing he wanted to do was to lie. So, he sat there and kept quiet.

Gaia also told them that time was running out and that they had to decide soon because they would need a month, at least, to age the children safely. "Dad, daddy, we need to do this; it's why we were created." Jory and Eric turned their heads and saw Christopher and Carmen standing behind them. Then, Marcus and Grace repeated Christopher's words.

It was Max who spoke first. Tears filled her eyes as she held James' hand while reaching for their kids. James let Max's hand go so she could take Marcus and Grace's hands. "I love both of you so very much. I know I have to trust you, but I'm scared. I don't want to see you hurt. I just want you safe and happy." Like normal kids, but she kept that thought to herself.

Max stood and eyed Gaia intently. "I'm not asking for much; the only thing I want is for the children to return home safely." Then she hugged and kissed Marcus and Grace and walked inside the house, shoulders shaking. James hugged and kissed the kids, and then he went inside as well.

Now, all eyes were on Eric and Jory. "Dad, daddy, it's time," Christopher said in a soft but determined voice as he hugged and kissed Jory and then Eric. Carmen did the same. After that, the children took Gaia's hand, but they didn't disappear. Instead, they waited until Eric and Jory were inside, then Gaia and the children vanished, followed by Destiny, and Chaos was the last to disappear. Before Chaos disappeared, he had eyed Eric and Jory intently, his expression unreadable.

Chapter Four

"Why is it taking so long?" Max growled. It had been ten days since Gaia had taken the children. "I don't know," Jory answered. James and Max were staying at the ranch just in case. The pack was worried as well; Jory could tell because they came by more often, asking about the children.

Eric and Jory had decided to let the pack know what was happening and why the children weren't at the ranch. "So, when they return, even Marcus and little Grace will be older than me?" Jake questioned, unbelief clear on his face.

Jake had been forced to join the attack on the Wentworth Pack by a group of rogue shifters. Their leader was known as Sam's former alpha. However, Jake refused to kill anyone, and soon after, he was accepted into the pack. Unfortunately, Jake's parents were murdered, and Eric had always suspected Hall Sanders, his former alpha, of ordering the hit.

"I'm afraid so," Eric chuckled. "Well, that sucks," he mumbled as he left to take care of the horses. Jory was a bit worried about the reaction of the pack and their friends since they weren't part of the whole ordeal. They would stay put and continue their daily routine.

Jory was curious how the pack would react to an adult Christopher and Carmen. The boy had left as a toddler and would return as a grown man. It was the same with Carmen; she would return as a young woman.

Jory eyed Eric; he said, "I wonder what they will look like when they finally return." Max's eyes lit up for the first time since they had arrived at the ranch. "I haven't thought of that. But, now that you mention it, how will Marcus and Grace look as grown-ups?" she said.

A bright light appeared, and a second later, Gaia stood in front of them. "It's time," she softly said as four pairs of eyes looked up at her expectantly. Gaia's voice was soothing and mesmerizing. "I have your word that the ranch and the pack are protected while we're away?" the alpha questioned. Gaia nodded; she assured Eric that Chaos would see to it personally that the pack's safety was guaranteed.

"Can we see the children?" Jory asked. "Unfortunately, I can't permit that. We don't want to disturb the process because that could get dangerous for the children," Gaia said. She looked thoughtful, nodded, and said, "The children's bodies are completed, and they will sleep for six days. On the second day of sleep, we will start to feed them their memories." Gaia paused and cocked her head as a sign that she was listening.

"Since you consented to age the children, we will share some secrets. Destiny, Chaos, and I formed a triumvirate," Gaia paused again, eying them intently. Finally, it was Jory who spoke. "Why did you form a triumvirate?"

"It was the only way to age the children and give them their memories. Chaos is powerful beyond anything we know, as you unquestionably can imagine. Even so, he needs Destiny and me to complete our task. Furthermore, after it is done, it's crucial that we protect the children as well as we can. As you know, Dhidysus and Leldur gained a lot of power, but it's Zachariah we have to watch out for," Gaia explained.

"Surely, Zachariah isn't more powerful than you or Chaos?" Eric questioned. "Even though I don't know where Zachariah is, I felt his power. And, unfortunately, that is not all because the moment I felt his power, I felt that of Leldur and Dhidysus as well," she looked from Max to James to Eric and let her gaze rest on Jory.

"Oh no," Jory looked horrified. "I'm afraid so," Gaia softly said. "What is it, baby?" the alpha said because he didn't like his mate's expression. Jory eyed Eric. "It means that Dhidysus, Leldur, and Zachariah probably have formed a triumvirate as well, thus triple their powers," he explained. "That's bad," Eric replied. "Yes, it certainly is," the alpha mate said.

"That's the second reason we had to establish a triumvirate. Even if we hadn't needed it to age the children, after those three idiots joined forces, we had to create a triumvirate to keep the universe balanced. So, we practically were forced into it, and for that reason alone, Chaos will have Zachariah's head and that of Dhidysus and Leldur," Gaia said; even though her tone was gentle, Jory could hear the anger.

"Why is Chaos so angry about them forming a triumvirate? You formed one as well, so you should be more powerful, right?" Eric said. "I don't think that's the issue," Jory said as he looked at his mate. "Once someone forms a triumvirate, they can't undo it again. A triumvirate is for life. So now Gaia, Destiny, and Chaos will be connected for eternity," he explained after seeing Eric's questionable look. "Damn," the alpha cursed. "Yep," Jory agreed.

"We really need to go now because time is not on our side," Gaia urged. "Can we see the children?" Max tried again. "No, because that's not a good idea. They are adults now and not the little ones you know. So letting you see them could harm not only the children but you as well. It will affect your memories, and that's the last thing we want," Gaia insisted.

"Why? I'm their mother," Max insisted. Gaia's expression softened even more when she said, "It would mess with your future memories, and you could go insane. To give someone new memories is very tricky; it's why we rarely do it."

Max sighed but finally relented. Jory and Eric also wanted to see Carmen and Christopher, but they knew that Gaia was right. The last thing they wanted was to put the children or themselves in danger. Gaia told them to hold hands and not let go, no matter what they felt. So, they did as they were told, and a moment later, they were in a room with four beds. The room was beautiful; the walls were off-white, and the four beds were of dark wood, or at least it seemed so. On the left wall, above two beds, hung a photograph of Christopher and Carmen.

On the right side of the room also stood two beds, and it had pictures of Marcus and Grace above the headrest.

Even though the room had no windows, it wasn't depressing. Instead, Eric, Jory, James, and Max somehow felt immediately at ease. Gaia smiled warmly, "I see that you like the room," she said.

"I guess that this is it," Jory said. "Yes, it is," Gaia softly replied, then she continued, "First, I will put you into a deep sleep, which will last eight hours, then we will start giving you memories. After that, the four of you will simultaneously wake up at the ranch. The children will follow shortly after we return you to the ranch."

"Do any of you have questions?" Gaia asked. "Yes, I have," the alpha mate replied. Gaia nodded. "How will you prepare the pack and our closest friends?" We will slightly alter their minds. "Destiny is at the ranch to explain things as we speak," Gaia informed them. That got the alpha's attention. "Why didn't you tell me about that? It's my duty as pack alpha to inform and prepare the pack. I don't want them to feel that I don't care," Eric muttered. It was obvious that Eric didn't like being kept in the dark.

"Destiny will explain why it's her who informs the pack, not their alpha and alpha mate. Because, as I said before, time is not our friend. So the longer we wait, the more power Zachariah gains," Gaia said patiently. "Then let's do it," Eric said. Jory nodded, and even James and Max nodded their okay.

Chapter Five

Eric opened his eyes and took in his surroundings. He turned his head sideways when he felt movement beside him. Jory was waking up slowly. They looked at each other, expressions serious. Neither of them made any move to get up. "This is strange," Jory whispered. "It is," Eric whispered back.

Gaia had returned Eric, Jory, Max, and James during the night after they had been away for six weeks. The children would follow soon, but it was of utmost importance that the four returned to the ranch because the pack needed their alpha. For a pack of werewolves, six weeks was a long time to go without their alpha.

It turned out that a neighboring pack wanted to take over the Wentworth Pack because their alpha was missing. When a pack loses its alpha, a new alpha must be chosen as soon as possible. However, Eric wasn't dead and hadn't abandoned his pack, so it was time to show that he was still alive and kicking.

"I hope the children will soon be here again; I miss them so much," Jory whispered as he leaned over Eric and pulled him close for a kiss. Eric softly moaned as he felt Jory's erection against his body. "I need you to claim me again," the alpha mate panted. "I know," Eric whispered.

The alpha grabbed Jory and flipped them so his mate was underneath him. "God, I love you so much," Eric whispered as he gently began to stroke the hard length of his panting mate. "Yes, I need you so much," Jory replied as he cupped Eric's face. Their eyes met while Eric continued stroking Jory's erection, which was producing a steady stream of precum.

Then, the alpha spread Jory's legs and gently started probing his mate's entrance. His fingers were slick with precum, so he didn't need lubricant. Jory lifted his hips when Eric pushed two fingers inside. "Yes, that's what I need, don't be gentle," Jory moaned as he spread his legs wider to accommodate Eric.

Jory stiffened when Eric inserted a third finger. Eric stilled. "Are you okay? Did I hurt you, baby?" the alpha sounded worried. "No, it just. We weren't intimate for six weeks, and apparently, my body needs a second or two to adjust," the alpha mate explained. "I'm good now; continue," Jory added, and Eric did.

He stretched his mate with practiced ease. Jory protested when Eric redrew his fingers but moaned in appreciation when the alpha positioned his cock and slowly pushed inside. Jory started to move his hips, and soon they moved in unison. Eric began kissing Jory while the alpha mate wrapped his hand around his stiff shaft and began stroking himself.

"Oh, baby, you're so beautiful, and you're mine, all mine," Eric growled as he quickened his pace. Jory knew that the alpha was ready to claim him. "Do it, babe," Jory demanded. That was all Eric needed to drive him over the edge. He lost what little control he had, leaned toward Jory's neck, and struck. Eric moaned as his mate's warm life essence flooded his mouth.

The alpha mate felt hot sperm burn his insides. Too long without sex had more impact on his body than Jory had anticipated. Jory was bucking underneath the alpha, hands fisting the sheets as he climaxed as well. Creamy warm semen splashed between their bodies.

Eric lay on his back, Jory next to him, his head resting on the mate's broad chest. The alpha had his arm around Jory's shoulders and squeezed him gently. Neither said anything, just enjoying the afterglow.

Yelling woke Jory and Eric. "What the hell?" the alpha growled as he jumped out of bed, Jory hot on his heels.

"Doug, you're trespassing again. I want you off the property," Dorian stood on the porch, hands folded over his chest, legs apart. When they had returned to the ranch the previous night, the alpha had let his pack know that he was back and that he and Jory were fine. This morning the pack would gather at the house, and Eric would fill them in about what they had experienced during the six weeks they had been away from the ranch.

Eric, who had stayed out of sight, saw that several shifters had taken position, ready to attack. Shit, because this was not good, and it was the last thing they needed right now. Eric knew that Dorian was able to handle Doug. His pack land was right next to Eric's, Doug had trespassed more than once, and Eric had it with the shifter. "Yeah, well, since your pack doesn't have an alpha anymore, I decided to take over and claim everything that comes with it," he said menacingly.

Dorian laughed because he knew that, even though he hadn't seen Eric yet, he knew that the alpha and his mate were back. "What if I don't leave?" Doug said defiantly. "Then, I'll make you," Eric said as he and Jory came to stand behind Dorian. "Welcome back, my friend," Dorian smiled. "It's good to be back. But, first, let's kick some ass because I'm fed up with this piece of shit," Eric growled. "Yes, please," Dorian grinned evilly.

Using their mind link, Jory silently asked if Eric would need his help, but the alpha declined. "Alright, Doug, bring it on," Eric's grin was one of pure evil, and Jory saw Doug pale as Mike, Billy, Jesse, Jordan, and even Jake blocked the only escape route.

Eric growled, and then the fight was on. Eric changed mid-air into his regular wolf form. Doug, who wasn't able to change as quickly as Eric, stayed human, and when Eric attacked, he pulled a gun aimed and, to Jory's horror, fired four bullets in rapid succession. And, what had never thought possible, happened right before his eyes; the alpha went down.

The moment Eric and Jory had returned to the ranch, Chaos had pulled back because now that he was back, Eric would take over his pack again. It shouldn't have been a problem for Eric to fight and kill Doug, but no one had considered that Doug had bullets that were lethal to a shifter, even a powerful one like Eric.

"NOOOO. ERIC," the alpha mate went to his knees to check Eric. The others were fighting Doug's soldiers, as the idiot called them, but the growling and sounds of flesh getting ripped apart stilled when Jory screamed his rage to the heavens. He glared at Doug, who turned and ran.

"No, he's mine," Jory said in a deep voice he didn't recognize as his own. "You take care of these bastards." Jory's following words shocked the pack to the core. "Kill them all." "Are you sure?" Dorian asked. "They tried to kill Eric, so yes, I'm sure. They started this mess, not me," the alpha mate replied, then he was gone. He knew that Sarah would take care of Eric.

Doug, in the meantime, had shifted and ran for his life because he knew he had gone too far. A shocked Doug skidded to a halt when Jory materialized in front of him. "Change back, coward," Jory commanded, his voice almost inhumane, low, and menacing. Even though an alpha himself, Doug couldn't do anything other than obey.

Jory looked disgusted at the slow transformation; this was so alpha unworthy. "You have a choice. Either you tell me the truth about why you attacked Eric, and I'll end your miserable life fast. Lie to me, and I will kill you very slowly. And make no mistake about it because as a magical creature, I have the means to do so," Jory said, his voice still unrecognizable.

The hate in Doug's eyes could melt the North Pole, but it meant nothing to what the alpha mate felt. All Jory wanted were answers because the attack didn't make sense. Doug should know that he would never be able to overpower the Wentworth Pack. The pack had angels, an archangel, witches, and even Ares, God of War, on their side. So, why would he be foolish enough to even try?

Doug, the coward that he was, began begging for his life. Jory, however, was adamant. "Talk, or face the consequences," he growled. "Someone approached me when I was in town. He said that he knew I hated Alpha Wentworth and that he had special bullets that would kill the alpha." Doug fell quiet, but Jory knew that there was more. "Talk," he commanded. Jory pushed his power into Doug, which meant that Doug had to obey Jory's every command.

"This man promised me fifty thousand dollars if I managed to kill or even weaken the alpha," he admitted in disgust. "Who gave you the bullets?" the alpha mate questioned; he needed an answer quickly because of what Doug had said. Even weakening Eric would be enough to launch a serious attack on the pack. "I honestly don't know. Please, please, don't kill me. I don't want to die," Doug pleaded. Jory pointed at Doug; the shifter was dead before falling to the ground.

Jory waved his hand over Doug, and the body disappeared. Then, he took his phone and dialed Dorian. "He?" The beta didn't get a chance to speak. "Dorian, listen. There will be a second attack, and this one will be more deadly. I'll explain when I get home. Keep our alpha safe," he said, then Jory hung up.

Chapter Six

Jory stood in the living room, where he saw Eric's lifeless body lying on the couch. "He's alive, but barely. I need to remove the bullets, but they are so many," Sarah, a trained nurse, said. "Son, you have healing powers, and now is the time to use them," Finn, a fallen angel, Sarah's mate, and Jory's biological father, softly said.

Jory knelt beside the couch and gently stroked Eric's blond curls. "Please, wake up, please?" he begged, but the alpha didn't move, his eyes closed. He placed both hands over his mate's chest and stomach and concentrated on the bullets. It was something he had never done before, but now was not the time to have second doubts. Eric's life was in danger, and Jory knew that If Eric died, not only he but their children would lose control. Jory would hunt down the perp if he had to destroy the earth to do it.

Then there were Christopher and Carmen. How would they react to the death of their beloved father? Jory shuddered; he forced all the negative thoughts to the back of his mind, concentrating on their love for each other and their children, who would soon come home.

Jory concentrated on the metal in Eric's chest and stomach again. He managed to extract seven bullets. What the hell? How had that even been possible? Doug shouldn't have the chance to fire more than one bullet into Eric. Jory had only heard four shots being fired. What the hell? How had that bastard managed to fire seven times? Sweet hell.

The alpha mate felt the energy drain as he forced the metal out of Eric's body. However, no rest for the wicked; he had to save his mate because without him? No, he wouldn't go there. Eric would pull through, Jory would not let Eric go, he would not.

"Here, sweetheart, drink this," Annabella, a witch, and Jory's mother said as she handed him a glass that had a greenish liquid in it. The alpha mate didn't question it because he trusted his mother. He took the glass and drank all of it. "Close your eyes for a couple of minutes," Annabella urged, and Jory did. The moment he closed his eyes, he felt his body glow, then he felt energy like he had never felt before, entering his body and mind.

A few minutes passed, and Jory opened his eyes. Annabella smiled. "I knew it would work. My special potion always works," she said. "Now, my child, do what you must do to heal Eric," the witch said.

So, Jory placed his hands over the still bleeding wounds, closed his eyes, and pushed all the power he could muster into the gaping holes. What seemed like days to Jory probably only lasted minutes. The alpha mate felt all of his energy leave him fast. He knew that healing took a lot of energy, but this wasn't good; something was wrong. "What's happening?" was all Jory managed to croak before the room tilted and his world went black.

Jory opened his eyes and frowned because he was lying on his back in a flower field, and he immediately knew where he was, Gaia's backyard, as he had called it, after arriving for the first time. "Why am I here?" he asked; his voice was normal again and he felt rested as well. "You were exhausting yourself to the point of no return," Gaia said.

"I don't understand," Jory replied. What did she mean by no return? Gaia smiled, and Jory was glad to see that it was a genuine one because it reached her beautiful eyes. "You were draining yourself too much. I felt the energy leaving you, and when I feel something like that happen, it's serious. You were so focussed on saving Eric that you didn't notice that your energy level was below zero. If I hadn't stopped you, then your brain would have suffered a loss of oxygen because you took too much energy. Eric's wounds are too severe for you to handle on your own, which means you need Christopher," Gaia explained.

"I need to go back; I can't let Eric die," Jory insisted. "We will not let the alpha die," said a voice Jory didn't recognize. "Jory, this is Clotho. She's one of the three fates. Clotho spins the thread of life. This thread will keep Eric alive. "And I'm Lachesis, and I assign each person a thread. I just assigned an extra one to Eric," the second woman, who had appeared right after Clotho.

That thought eased Jory somewhat. "There are three of you?" Clotho nodded. "That would be correct," she said. "Where is the third one?" the alpha mate questioned. "Right now, we don't need her because Atropos snips the thread of life at its very end. And we don't want that," Clotho explained. Jory nodded because it would mean losing Eric, which was not an option.

"Close your eyes," Gaia softly said. Jory did as he was told and sighed deeply when he felt calm, pure energy flow into his body and mind. "You can open your eyes again. You're ready to go back to the ranch. But before I let you go, you need to know a few things," Gaia said. Jory looked intently at Mother Earth, waiting for her to continue.

"We will take care of Eric, and to do that, we don't need to descend to earth. So, don't try and heal your mate because it won't help him and will do you no good. There will be another attack on the ranch. Dhidysus and Leldur want Christopher, but the fools don't know that the children are with us. Even if we told them, they wouldn't believe us. And, since Eric cannot defend the pack, you have to step in," Gaia gently explained.

"But, I thought that you had them locked up. How could they escape?" Jory was stunned because Gaia, and Destiny, together with Chaos, should be able to keep Leldur and Dhidysus restrained, right? "We don't know how it happened, but as you can imagine, Chaos is beside himself with rage. They must have had help, and we will find out who that was. That person or persons will pay dearly," she said. Jory frowned and looked thoughtful because it seemed like Gaia was angry. And, if there was one thing that Mother Earth didn't do, it was getting angry. So, this meant that whatever was going on had to be huge.

Jory was silent for a long time because he needed time to comprehend what Gaia had told him. How can I step up? I'm not an alpha. Plus, I need to watch over Eric because he's unconscious and can't defend himself." Jory exclaimed, skeptically eyeing Gaia, Clotho, and Lachesis. "I don't know how to keep the pack and our friends safe. I'm not Eric," he whispered.

"No, you're not Eric, that's true. However, you are a magical creature and extremely powerful in your own right. You're part angel and part witch. Your mother, Annabella, is a mighty witch, as is your grandmother, Cassandra. And I didn't even mention your grandfather, Ares, God of War. So, Jory Wentworth Bradshaw, you should be able to defend the pack and everyone who lives there." Gaia paused and looked at Jory before she let both hands hover over the alpha mate's head and shoulders. "Yes, there's a lot of magic inside you. Trust your magic," she said. Jory was back at the ranch in the blink of an eye. All pack members, angels, an archangel, and even the God of War were eyeing him in wonder. "Where have you been?" Dorian questioned. "How is he?" Jory asked Sarah, ignoring Dorian.

"The same. I think that he's stable," she softly said. Jory knelt beside the couch and tenderly stroked the alpha's cheeks. Then, he turned and eyed Dorian. "Gaia summoned me because apparently, I drained myself of too much energy. She said that if she hadn't stopped me, my brain would eventually have suffered from loss of oxygen."

"How is that possible?" Dorian questioned. "It seemed I lost focus when I tried to heal Eric," I explained. "Oh, shit." "What is it?" Jesse asked. "Gaia told me that soon Dhidysus and Leldur will attack the ranch. They are after Christopher and don't know he's not here anymore," Jory replied while he took Eric's hand. He needed physical contact. Hell, he needed his mate. He leaned toward Eric's ear and whispered, "It will be alright. Everything will be fine."

"What about Eric? We can't leave him here," JJ said. "Yes, we can. He's under the protection of not only Gaia but the three fates as well. They promised to keep him safe, and I trust them," the alpha mate said. Jory sighed, kissed Eric, and told the pack to prepare for battle.

"That's good enough for me," Dorian said as he began to order the pack, readying them for battle.

Chapter Seven

Annabella and Cassandra were drawing powerful wards at every window and door. Billy, Jesse, Mike, and Devon would shift, and the rest would stay human. Finn had made it clear that he wouldn't leave Sarah's side. Alex, Rose, and baby Caitlin were at James and Max's place. Jory had sent Max home; he had tried to send James home as well, but the sheriff had insisted he stay and defend the ranch. If it came down to it, Max, together with Alex, would help protect Rose and Caitlin.

"Holy hell," JJ whispered as a powerful fireball smashed against the living room window. Even though it happened fast, Armand was able to pull JJ away from the window even faster. The window was holding, but Cassandra knew it wouldn't last long if they kept throwing fireballs against it.

"That was at the back of the house," Finn yelled when there was an explosion that shook the house. The noise was deafening, and then all hell broke loose. The house was attacked from all sides, which would have been impossible if it were just Leldur and Dhidysus. "Who the hell is aiding them," Jory growled. The alpha mate cursed when he heard the dogs whine. He turned to see the four dogs cowering in the corner by the fireplace. "Felicia, would you?" "Of course," she said. The fallen angel touched the blanket, covering them in bright white twinkling lights, then they were gone. Jory sighed in relief, which was short-lived when three fireballs simultaneously hit the living room window.

Jory saw the pack members who had shifted, rushing outside, and then the fight was on. Lots of growling, and the alpha mate saw red when Billy was attacked by three rogue shifters. He didn't even notice that his eyes had begun to glow when he lifted his arms. Then, with outstretched arms and his fingers spread, Jory unleashed his magnificent but very deadly blue fire.

How he managed not to hit Billy, Jory didn't know. But, it was like the blue streak of fire knew that Billy was pack and not to hurt him. The three rogues lay dead on the ground, and it was then that Jory saw blood gushing out of the deep wounds on Billy's side and hind leg.

"I'll take him to the house," Finn said. "I'll cover you," Armand said, and then bright twinkling light appeared and took the two angels. A minute later, Finn carried an unconscious and severely wounded Billy into the living room. "Come with me," Sarah said. Finn didn't question his mate but followed her. Jory knew that Sarah would put Billy in the first guestroom because it was turned into a mini hospital.

The alpha mate didn't want to leave the room, but he had to know how Billy was doing. "It's not good; we need Jack," Sarah informed him. "Consider it done," said Jory as he left the room. He needed Armand to get Jack, but he wasn't sure if the angel would leave JJ. "Armand?" he called, and a second later, he saw the angel appear, JJ at his side.

"Yes, Jory. What's up?" the angel questioned. "I need you to get Jack." Before Armand could answer, JJ said, "Just do it. I'm not made out of glass, and I can defend myself. I'm half shifter and half vampire. It will be okay." "I don't like leaving you here with the battle going on." "The sooner you leave to pick up Jack, the sooner you'll be back," JJ insisted.

Armand nodded, kissed JJ, and then he reluctantly orbed away. "Thank you," Jory said. JJ frowned. "For what?" he said. "For making Armand go and fetch Jack. I didn't want to ask Finn again because he already did so much," the alpha mate explained. "Ah, well, Armand thinks I'm still the same helpless kid he met two years ago," JJ replied. But before Jory could say more, the house shook again.

"I need to see if everyone is still alright," Jory said as he rushed down the stairs. "The windows are holding for now, but I don't know for how long," Annabella informed her son. "We need to strengthen the wards again," Cassandra insisted. "Let's try if we can manage it without getting killed," Annabella replied. "Be careful, please?" Jory urged.

The two witches nodded, and then they started working on the wards. Just when they were about to renew the ward in the living room, the one that had gotten the most fireballs, another ball of fire was thrown their way. Both women moved to the side, just in case the window wouldn't hold. Luckily the wards still were powerful enough.

Cassandra and Annabella eyed each other. "We need to hurry," Cassandra urged. "Absolutely," Annabella agreed. So, they hurried to strengthen the existing wards and added two extra wards. Then, they went from window to window and door to door while the pack was still fighting, defending the house. Then Jory saw Evan being attacked by four rogues. "God damn, this is so not fair," he muttered as he opened the front door and went outside, ready to jump into the fray.

Two rogues had jumped Evan's back; one was attacking from behind, and the fourth was fighting Evan from the front. The alpha mate extended his claws and growled when he saw Evan losing the battle. But, just when the rogue went for Evan's jugular, Jory grabbed him by the throat.

"You dare to touch one of mine?" he said in a voice that was foreign to him, right before he tore the shifter's head from its torso and threw it away. Then he looked around, and it felt like he was looking down from the balcony. Evan looked up, eyes huge, and then he smiled through the pain. "You grew quite a bit in the last few minutes," the shifter panted.

Jory didn't understand, but it was then that he noticed the fighting had stopped, and everyone was staring at him. Jory eyed the battlefield and was enraged when he saw his pack was wounded. Evan couldn't walk because the wounds had weakened him. Jesse's side was ripped open, and blood was gushing from the deep wound. Mike's hind leg was broken, and his ear nearly ripped from his head. James had taken down two rogues, but five others had attacked him. As a result, he had a deep cut on his shoulder and right side. Then there was Billy; Jory didn't even know how he was doing. God, what a mess; he hadn't been able to keep the pack safe.

Rage, which he'd rarely felt, filled him as he lifted his arms, pointed his hands at the rogues and released his fire. Within seconds it was over, and the rogues were no more than a small pile of ashes. Suddenly he felt drained, which was precisely what they had warned him to watch out for. "Let's get him inside," Dorian said.

Once inside the house, Cassandra brewed a potion to replenish Jory's energy. "Sit and stay," Annabella said sternly. Jory frowned but did as he was told. He watched Eric, who still lay on the couch. Emma, Eric's sister, had told Jory that the alpha hadn't even stirred during the fighting and fireballs hitting the house. Jory looked up and silently mouthed a thank you.

Evan, Mike, and Jesse were treated for their wounds by Cassandra, Annabella, and Emma. "How is Billy doing?" Jory was afraid of the answer he would get, but still, he had to know. "Jack is still treating him. He lost a lot of blood, but he's strong and will pull through," Sarah said, gently smiling at him. Jory inhaled and exhaled and instantly felt better. No pack member had lost their lives, which was good. Now he needed Eric to regain consciousness and the children back at the ranch.

"What's wrong with him?" Dorian asked, pointing at Eric. He had wanted to ask sooner, but the attack had prevented that. "The wounds Eric has are severe, and I could only heal him partly. For him to heal completely, I need Christopher. But, since he's not available, we have to wait," the alpha mate explained. "What wounds? I don't see any?" Dorian said. "Eric has internal wounds. Gaia and the three fates are keeping him stable, or else he." Jory stopped talking because he couldn't say it. "I get it," Dorian softly said.

"Do you have any idea when the aging of the children will be completed?" Dorian questioned. Jory shook his head because he had no idea. "I hoped that by now, they would have brought the kids back, but unfortunately, they haven't," the alpha mate replied solemnly.

Jory turned when Jack entered the room. "Billy will be fine; all he needs is rest and fluids, lots of fluids," the jaguar said. "Let me look at the others," Jack added after seeing the wounded pack members. "Thank you," the alpha mate said as he knelt beside the couch and gently caressed Eric's cheek. "We need you, big guy. Stay strong; just hold on a bit longer, okay?" Jory whispered as he carefully kissed the alpha's chest.

Jory felt Eric weaken, praying his mate would hold on until Christopher was back. What a mess. What a fucking mess. Jory knew that if it had been any other shifter or alpha even, they would have died on the spot. Eric was a true alpha, and he was beyond powerful, which showed because the alpha's heartbeat was still strong, giving Jory hope. Eric had to pull through; he just had to.

Chapter Eight

"Dad?" Jory froze at hearing the familiar yet unknown voice. "Christopher," he whispered before he turned and had his arms full of two grown people. "Carmen, Christopher. You're home. We missed you so much. How are you? And?" Jory had so many questions. He was so stunned by the sudden return of his children that he hadn't even noticed their appearance.

It wasn't until Christopher and Carmen gently untangled themselves that Jory nearly fainted. "Let me look at you," he whispered in awe. In front of the alpha mate stood a beautiful young woman and a ruggedly handsome man. Carmen's hair was light brown, her eyes a pale green, and she was slender and about 5 foot 8.

Christopher was ruggedly handsome, with a sharp jawline and a straight nose that fit his face perfectly. His hair was at shoulder length and so black that, when the sun shone on it, his hair appeared dark blue. His eyes were the same color as Carmen's.

Jory smiled, he softly said, "I know what you would look like, but damn, it's so strange. You're not little anymore. It will take some time to get used to. I love the memories, though."

Christopher blushed. "Me too," he replied. "I'm sure that you have some private memories. The ones we parents are oblivious to?" the alpha mate chuckled. Christopher didn't answer. Then Jory turned to Carmen. "You've grown into a beautiful young woman. I like the color of your hair and eyes," Jory said as he hugged his son and daughter tightly.

Christopher looked uncertain when he said, "I need to ask one favor of you and father." "Anything," the alpha mate said. "As of now, I would like it if you called me Chris instead Christopher. I like the name, but Christopher was the little tyke, and I'm not that toddler anymore," Christopher explained. "No problem, Chris," Jory smiled. "Thanks, dad," Chris said, then added, "I know that father needs us. Gaia told us everything that went on while we were gone," Christopher said, and Jory could tell that his son wasn't happy.

"Come on, let's heal your father," the alpha mate said as he guided them up the stairs and into the bedroom. They stood next to each other at Eric's bedside. Jory gently stroked the alpha's hair. Chris, who stood next to him, touched his father's chest, careful not to touch the invisible gaping bullet wounds. Carmen let her hand rest on Eric's left knee and eyed Jory.

Everyone who looked at the alpha would see flawless skin; Chris, however, could see through that, and to him, the wounds were very much visible.

"I know," the alpha mate said when he saw the look in his daughter's eyes. Carmen wanted revenge for what was done to their father. Jory didn't doubt that Chris would search and find those responsible and would deal with them accordingly.

"Now, let us heal father, and then we celebrate our return, and we finally are reunited again," Chris said. Jory was all for that because even though he was protected by Gaia and the three fates, Eric was getting weaker by the day.

"How are we going to do this?" Jory questioned because he had no idea. "I need both of you to touch me because that way, we multiply my power," Chris said. Carmen and Jory touched Chris under his shirt so his arms would be free.

When Carmen and Jory touched Chris' skin, he stretched his arms, closed his eyes, and began to whisper words Jory couldn't decipher. It wasn't important right now because all Jory wanted was for Eric to regain consciousness. He wanted his mate in his arms again.

Jory felt Chris' body heat up. When he turned his head sideways to check on his son, he was flabbergasted to see that Chris was glowing.

However, it wasn't a red glow like Jory's, but an eerie greenish color. Carmen looked normal; no, she too began to glow.

If Jory hadn't been so used to magic to heal someone, he would have run for the hills, screaming bloody murder. Chris let his hands hover over Eric's body, murmured some incoherent words, and slowly levitated the alpha.

Eric began to glow even brighter than Chris, who started to shake. "I need you, dad," he whispered. Jory knew instinctively what to do as he closed his eyes and concentrated on his mate and son. He felt his magic flow into Chris, and Eric began to glow even brighter, nearly blinding Jory when he opened his eyes.

"Keep them closed, dad," Chris whispered. Jory didn't question his son but kept them closed. "I need more," Chris said after what seemed like forever. It appeared that Carmen knew what to do because without losing skin contact with her brother, she moved her hand toward Jory's. "Move your hand toward me," she urged, and Jory did as asked. The moment their hands touched, Eric began to toss and turn while still hovering.

The alpha mate felt the power surge through him and gasped because it took his breath away, literally. Jory tried not to show that breathing had become difficult. However, he felt Carmen squeezing his hand. The alpha mate didn't dare look at his daughter for fear of losing his concentration. Nothing mattered more than to heal Eric.

Chris had apparently noticed that his father had breathing problems because he suddenly moved his right hand and touched Jory's forehead. Breathing immediately got easier; when Jory's heartbeat slowed, Chris removed his hand and let it hover over Eric's chest again. Jory wanted to ask why it took so long to heal his mate, but he didn't want to disturb Chris in what he was doing. Finally, after what seemed like an eternity, Eric slowly opened his eyes. "Welcome back, baby," Jory whispered as he leaned toward his mate and gently kissed him on the forehead.

Jory knew he needed to inform Eric about everything that had happened while he was unconscious. So, he started explaining carefully. "Whoa, slow down, baby," Eric said as he sipped his water. "So, that idiot Doug wanted to take over my pack? What the hell was he thinking? Where is he now?" Eric spoke in a low and menacing voice, and he sounded furious. "They are dead," Dorian stated.

After Eric woke, they took the time to reunite with their daughter and son, talking about memories and how strange it was to have them. Even though Eric, Jory, Max, and James had received images of the different aging states, everyone was still in awe. There were even pictures of the children growing into adulthood. It was so familiar, yet so strange. Jory had tried to find the words to describe how he felt but failed miserably.

Eric had asked about Carmen's color of hair and her eyes. She had told him that Gaia had made them choose, and she wanted light brown hair and pale green eyes. "Well, it suits you, sweetheart," the alpha had complimented his now grown-up daughter.

Eric had been impressed that Jory had ordered to kill every single rogue who was in on the attack. He was even more stunned to hear that Jory had killed Doug. "Well, he shouldn't have fired those damn bullets at you. He deserved to die, and that scum was lucky that I made it quick," Jory stated. Eric's eyes shone with pride when he said, "You did well, baby. You acted like a real alpha." Then the alpha lifted Jory's face and kissed him tenderly on his full, kissable lips, making his mate moan. That evening they celebrated that the children had returned to the ranch and that Eric had been healed.

However, Eric thought it was a pity that the rogues were dead because he would have loved getting his claws on them. "Well, you can brace yourself because soon Dhidysus and Leldur will attack because they want Chris. Only, they don't know that our boy is a grown man," Jory chuckled.

"Let them come; I can't wait," Chris growled. "Me neither," Carmen chimed in. Eric and Jory both looked surprised at hearing Carmen speak like that. "I mean it, dad. It's time they know to leave us in peace or face the consequences," Carmen said. And they all knew what Carmen meant.

Jory knew that his daughter had special powers. Carmen was able to amplify Chris' powers, making him almost invincible. Suddenly Carmen looked from Eric to Jory and said, "Oh, did I mention Gaia's gift?" Both men eyed their daughter, confused expressions on their faces. "By the looks you give me, I would say no. Well, anyway, she told me that I was ready to command nature," Carmen said it so matter of factly, it was almost comical, almost.

Eric raised one eyebrow. "Did she teach you how to handle this gift safely?" he questioned. "She sure did," Carmen replied, smiling. "I had to make a vow never to abuse my gift. I took the vow, and after that, she did something, and I received my gift," she explained. "Oh, I already practiced while Chris and I were undergoing the aging process," she added.

"Oh, dad, daddy, I'm so happy to be back again. I missed you and the pack and our friends so much," Carmen said, hugging Eric and Jory tightly. "We missed you too, sweetheart," Jory said as his eyes filled with unshed tears. But, he would not cry; he would not!

The days passed without incidents, and life at the ranch almost felt normal again, if only there weren't the threat of Dhidysus and Leldur. Then, there was the question of who had aided Doug in attacking the pack with the intent of taking over. And, it was probable that that same person had sold Doug the special bullets that would bring even a true alpha down.

As if reading his mate's thoughts, and maybe he had, Jory squeezed Eric's knee; he said, "We will get them eventually, no worries, babe."

Chapter Nine

"What you did for me was huge. You drained yourself, hoping to heal me and save my life," the alpha softly said. "I love you. You're my mate, and I just wanted you to get better," Jory replied in an equally soft voice.

It was after midnight, and Eric and Jory still were talking about their children and what had happened. Also, they needed to prepare for another attack, and this one would be much more deadly. Eric was convinced that Dhidysus and Leldur had recruited creatures to help them destroy the pack and take Christopher. The two fallen Gods were convinced that they were able to strip Christopher from his powers and use them for their personal gain.

There was a knock on the door, Jory called for their son to enter, and a moment later, Chris stepped into the room. "Hey, son, come and sit with us," Eric motioned for Chris to sit beside him on the edge of the bed.

"I can see that something is troubling you. Whatever it is, you know you can talk to us," Jory said. Chris looked thoughtful, and for a second, Jory thought that he would stay quiet, but then he said, "I don't understand why Dhidysus and Leldur still want to kidnap me. By now, they should be aware that we have aged. They weren't able to take me when I was a toddler, and they certainly won't be able to take me now. I have powers that are beyond imagination." Chris looked pained, opened his mouth to speak, hesitated, but finally said, "I'm even more powerful than the two of you combined."

That got Eric and Jory's attention. Of course, they knew their son would be extremely powerful once an adult. "I guess that you didn't know?" Chris questioned carefully. "No, we didn't. And I wonder why no one took the liberty to inform us," Eric said. He then eyed Chris intently, his gaze tender as he said, "It doesn't make any difference how powerful you are; to us, you'll always be our son who we love and respect. The same goes for Carmen, but she knows that." "I sure do, father," said Carmen, who was standing in the doorway, smiling.

She entered the bedroom and hugged Jory, then Eric before she sat on the edge of the bed next to Jory. Eric looked from one to the other. "Even though the bed is large, it's too small for four people to sit beside each other," the alpha chuckled.

"That's our cue to leave," Chris said as he rose from the bed and motioned for his sister to follow him. "Wait," Jory called after Chris. The man turned and looked in question at his dad. "You still haven't told us what's bothering you. And don't say that it's nothing because even though you've aged tremendously in a short amount of time, you're still our Christopher."

Carmen eyed Chris, and Jory suspected they were using their mind link to discuss things. "Guys, come on. Please don't talk so secretively because you know your father, and I don't like it," Jory said. It was true; he really didn't like it. The kids were connected by a unique link since they were little.

Jory was anxious to know what was bothering his son, so he called him back. Chris turned and eyed Eric and Jory for a long time. "You want me to stay?" Carmen offered. Chris shook his head because what he had to say wasn't meant for Carmen to hear. He didn't want to upset Carmen. And he knew that she would be upset if she knew what he was about to tell his two dads.

Chris sighed, then sat down. He didn't make eye contact when he started to explain. "I don't know if it was planned by Gaia, but during the aging process, I had visions, and they terrified me."

"Oh sweetheart, what can be so terrifying that it upset you so much?" Jory spoke in a soothing voice, the same tone he had used to comfort Christopher when he still was a toddler. The alpha mate was a bit surprised to hear that Chris, their extremely mighty son, had a vision that had upset him. The vibes the alpha mate received from his son weren't reassuring. Chris seemed, well, afraid.

"What are you so afraid of, and what is upsetting you? Talk to us, please?" Jory gently urged. The door opened, and a worry-looking Carmen walked into the room. "If it's about my family, then I have a right to hear what you have to say," she stated. Eric and Jory looked at Chris because he had to decide if Carmen was allowed to stay.

"Stay, please?" Chris said in a barely audible voice. Carmen sat on the floor opposite the bed where Eric, Jory, and Chris were sitting. "As I said, during the aging process, I had a vision," Chris paused and sighed deeply before continuing. "In my vision, the two of you got killed."

Jory gasped, and Eric frowned. "We got murdered? How, and by whom?" Eric questioned. "That's the worst part because I was the one who killed you," Chris whispered. "I don't understand. You would never harm us. I refuse to believe that you would even think of murdering us," Jory stated firmly. He loved their children above everything else, and there was nothing he wouldn't do for them, or Eric, or the pack.

"I'm with my mate on this one," Eric said, turned to face Chris, and added, "Your dad and I trust you with our lives. That's a fact and won't change." "We need to know exactly what it was you saw, or you think you saw," Jory said because he didn't trust visions entirely. After all, they could easily be wrongly interpreted.

"It was here at the ranch. You and dad were busy tending the horses. I walked up and killed you," Chris whispered. Jory's heart broke when he saw the pain and devastation in his son's eyes. "We trust you, Chris. We know that you would never harm us in any way," Jory assured. "Son, whatever you saw, is wrong. That's why I don't trust visions. Whatever you think you saw is wrong," Jory insisted.

They talked for a long time before Chris went to his room. Then, when they were alone, they looked at each other, disbelieve written on both their faces. "Any thoughts?" Eric asked. Jory shook his head. "Not really. To be honest, I don't know what to think. The only thing I know is that Chris would never hurt us," the alpha mate replied.

"Tomorrow, we will inform the pack about Chris' vision because they have a right to know," Eric said as he pulled Jory close. Ever since he woke, they didn't have a moment to themselves. The alpha was still tired because, even though he was healed, his body needed a bit more time to regain its full strength.

"I agree, but we need to talk to Chris first because he has to be okay with it," Jory replied. "That goes without saying," the alpha said as he wrapped his arms around his mate, kissed his temple, and closed his eyes. He was so God damn tired.

It was after nine the following day when a knock on the door woke Eric and Jory. "Come in," the alpha mate called. A serious-looking Chris entered the room. The alpha and his mate sat up in alarm. "Everything is fine, no worries," Chris stated as he walked to the edge of the bed. "Sit," Jory petted the spot beside him.

"Are the two of you alright?" Chris inquired carefully. Both men frowned; it was Eric who answered. "Yes, son, we are fine. However, I think that we can't say the same regarding you." "That's because I'm not alright," Chris sounded tired and pained. The following words shocked both Eric and Jory. "It's okay if you want to inform the others about my vision. They deserve to know."

"How did you know we wanted to inform the pack about your vision?" Jory was stunned. Had Chris gained more powers than they assumed? Could it be that their son had received the gift of premonition?

Chris' smile was rueful when he said, "It is something that you would do. The vision I had is too important not to share with the pack and our friends." Chris squeezed Jory's shoulder; he added, "And, I know you would talk to me first about it. So, no, I don't have the gift of premonitions."

"So, you really don't mind if we inform the others about what you saw?" Eric questioned. "No, but I want to be present when you share my information," Chris replied. "Of course, son. We wouldn't want to have it any other way," the alpha said.

"I need coffee," Chris stated as he rose from the edge of the bed and moved to the door, which he silently closed after him.

"I'm worried because this isn't the Christopher we know. He almost seems depressed," Jory said. Eric nodded because that was precisely what he was thinking. "I believe he is not doing so great. We need to know what's going on because we won't let anything happen to Chris," a grim-looking Eric replied.

"They better leave him alone because I will destroy everyone who tries to harm him," Jory growled. Eric didn't have an answer to that because he knew that his mate had the power to destroy the earth. He only hoped that it wouldn't come to it. "Let's get dressed; I need coffee," Eric quietly said.

Chapter Ten

"Are you sure that it really was you?" Dorian asked. The beta was flabbergasted at hearing about Chris' vision. It was evident that he couldn't believe that Chris would actually hurt his two dads. "Positive," Chris quietly answered.

Eric and Jory had called a pack meeting, which meant family and friends were present. Some had gasped, and others silently observed Chris. "Did you feel anything when you saw yourself killing Eric and Jory? I'm asking this because it could be important," Dacian, the archangel, gently questioned.

Chris frowned; he didn't look happy. "Are you accusing me of?" He didn't get the chance to finish his sentence. "No no. Absolutely not. I'm just trying to find out how credible your vision is. What you might not know is that one, if powerful enough, can tamper with visions. For example, a mighty warlock could have fed you the images of you murdering your dads. It doesn't say that it's true," the archangel explained calmly.

That got everyone's attention. "Tell us what you know about tampering with the mind of others. I find it hard to believe that someone was able to feed Chris some bullshit misinformation," Eric said. Jory looked thoughtful, and it was the alpha mate who spoke. "It could be possible because, during the aging, the minds of all four of you were vulnerable. So if someone was powerful enough, they could have put the image in Chris' mind."

"Could it really be that the children were susceptible to influences from the outside during the time they were sleeping?" Billy quietly asked. "We need to ask Gaia because she's the only one who can answer that," Jory replied. Only Gaia couldn't be summoned, like angels and demons. Jory knew he would need total concentration on letting Mother Earth know that he was desperate and needed information only she could provide.

The alpha mate had retreated to his bedroom and told everyone not to disturb him because he needed complete focus on contacting Gaia. Jory didn't know how long he had been in the bedroom when the door slowly opened, and Eric peeked inside.

"How are things going, baby?" the alpha softly inquired. Jory shook his head. "Not like I had hoped. It doesn't matter how hard I try; it's almost as if something or someone is blocking me," he said. Eric stepped into the room and sat on the bed beside his mate. He cupped Jory's face, their eyes met, and the alpha was surprised by the pain and worried expression he saw on Jory's face.

Eric pulled Jory close and gently kissed him on the eyes, nose, and mouth. The alpha mate parted his lips and welcomed Eric's hot tongue. They wrapped their arms around each other, and both men intensified the kiss. Eric was about to undress his sexy mate when Jory pulled back. Before Eric could even ask if everything was alright, Jory disappeared. "Gaia," the alpha mumbled.

Jory opened his eyes and immediately knew where he was when he saw the flowers surrounding him. A moment later, Gaia materialized. She smiled gently down at him. "What is troubling you so bad that you need me?" her voice was soft and soothing.

Jory sighed as he pushed himself upright before rising to his feet. "I want you to explain the aging process once again because something is wrong with Chris," he said. The alpha mate was cautious because Gaia wasn't someone who took being summoned lightly. Well, it was a kind of summoning because Gaia herself decided if she wanted to grant someone an audience. Mother Earth could not be summoned; no one, not even Chaos, who had created her, could command her to see him. Nevertheless, she seemed to have a soft spot for Jory because she had never refused him anything.

Gaia looked confused. "Explain," she said, and Jory did. He told her about Chris' vision and that no one could imagine Chris hurting his dads. Jory explained that Dacian had told them that visions could be tampered with. So, now they suspected that someone powerful enough had invaded Chris' mind.

Gaia looked thoughtful, and for the first time, Jory saw anger in her eyes. Shit, this wasn't good. She shook her head. "That shouldn't have been possible, but," Gaia paused, closed her eyes, and a moment later, Destiny materialized. "What's wrong?" she asked, looking from Jory to Gaia and back to Jory again. It was evident that she hadn't expected to see the alpha mate so soon again.

Gaia explained what Jory had told her, and the alpha mate could see the disbelief on Destiny's face. "I don't understand," she softly said, looking confused. "This shouldn't be possible. Because that would mean that the security shield was breached, which should be impossible," Destiny added.

Gaia closed her eyes and, to Jory's astonishment, became nearly translucent. Destiny, however, didn't seem worried, so Jory supposed that she had seen Gaia getting translucent before. He wanted to ask Destiny what Gaia was doing, but one look from her and the alpha mate knew he had to wait.

Mother Earth nearly disappeared completely before regaining her solid form again. She looked thoughtful, and Jory could tell that she wasn't happy. He wanted her to urge sharing her thoughts but knew it wouldn't be wise to insist. So he waited patiently until Gaia would enlighten them.

"What did you discover?" Destiny asked. Gaia looked troubled; she said, "It's possible someone breached the protection," she informed them. "Oh, that's not good," Destiny replied, looking thoughtful. "No, it's not."

It was a relief that the possibility was there that someone could have messed with Chris' mind. Being a powerful magical creature himself, Jory knew that messing with someone's mind was very tricky and dangerous. But then, rage filled him, and whoever had messed with his son's mind would pay with their lives.

"Could you sense who it was that possibly breached the protection dome?" Jory questioned. He couldn't wait to get his hands on the ones who had dared to touch his son, who had been in his most vulnerable state. "Unfortunately, no. There was a magical weak spot, but there was nothing that indicated that someone had tampered with it," Gaia said.

That was strange because Jory knew Gaia herself had provided the protection dome surrounding the sleeping children. "So, how can we determine if the vision was tampered with?" Jory questioned. Gaia sighed, and Jory's heart sank when he saw Gaia's expression.

"There's no way to find out someone messed with Chris' mind. I'm sorry, but you will have to wait and see. I know it won't be easy, but for now, there's not much else we can do," Gaia explained. Well, Jory refused to believe that Chris would turn on them. The alpha mate knew that his time with Gaia was up.

He opened his eyes and saw that he was back at the ranch again. All eyes were on him when he entered the living room. Chris looked uncertain. Carmen was the first to hug him. Eric smiled as he took his mate in his arms and kissed him.

Still in Eric's arms, Jory eyed Chris. "Whatever happens, we believe in you. You are our son, and we know that you will never harm us, no matter what happens," he stated firmly. "So, I assume that you didn't get any wiser?" Chris asked.

Jory shook his head because it was the truth. "No, not really. But Gaia found a magical weak spot in the barrier that was made to protect you while you were aging. However, she couldn't tell if anyone had indeed penetrated the shield. So, technically it's possible that someone managed to breach the protection and got to you," Jory said. He knew that it was a long shot but not impossible.

"Whatever happens, we have faith in you, my son. That means we need to find the one who planted that shitty vision into your mind," Eric growled. "Thank you, dad," Chris was visibly relieved after hearing that the pack and their friends had faith in him. "We will get that SOB," Carmen said as she hugged her brother.

Chapter Eleven

"Is everything alright?" Carmen asked her brother. Chris, who stood in front of the floor-to-ceiling windows, looked over his shoulder. He considered Carmen for a few seconds. "I'm worried about the vision or premonition I had," he answered as he turned his face toward the window again.

"I think our dads are right; someone planted that vision into your brain. Whoever managed to invade your mind must be very powerful," Carmen said. Chris nodded while he kept staring out of the window. "Remember that you're not alone," said another voice. "I know, Marcus," Chris softly replied. "You know we stand by you until the end, right?" Grace said. Marcus and Grace had felt Chris' despair and had immediately rushed to the ranch.

"Where are your dads?" Grace inquired. "Out, riding. Quality time and all that," Carmen answered. "They left you all by yourself?" Grace was stunned because Eric and Jory hadn't given Chris any privacy since they knew about the vision. Then, there was the attack they'd been warned about, but it hadn't happened so far. The waiting had them on edge because three weeks had gone by without a trace of Dhidysus and Leldur.

All the waiting had brought on a lot of tension, and Eric and Jory hadn't left Chris' side even for a moment. "We had a disagreement the previous day because I was fed up with them being my shadows. I mean, I couldn't even shower without dad or father guarding the door," Chris sighed.

"They love you, and that's why they are so protective," Grace said. "I know, but still. They should know by now that I'm perfectly able to defend myself. I always could, ever since I was a baby," Chris said.

The alpha and his mate stepped into the room. "Back so soon?" Chris said, and he didn't sound happy. "Yes, because we encountered Dhidysus while on our way to the pond," Eric explained. The alpha used his soothing tone because he didn't want to antagonize his son any further.

That got Chris' attention; he turned away from the window and eyed his dads. "What happened? Are the two of you alright?" a concerned Chris asked. "Yes, we're fine. But unfortunately, he got away before we could kill him," Jory said. Then, Eric explained how they were on their way to the pond when Dhidysus materialized in front of them. Eric glanced at Jory, smiled, and added. "If my dear mate hadn't reacted as fast as lightning, he would have surely wounded us."

"I threw some blue fire at him, but he disappeared just as suddenly as he appeared. I didn't know that he could be so quick," Jory said. Chris looked thoughtful; he said, "I'm convinced they have help from a powerful being. All we need to do is find out who is aiding them and destroy that person." "Dacian is following Dhidysus's trace as we speak," Eric informed Chris, Carmen, Marcus, and Grace.

"Don't tell me that the idiot was so stupid to leave a magical trace," Marcus said. But before Eric could answer, they heard James and Max drive up to the house. "Oops, we forgot to tell them we are here," Marcus chuckled. "Yep and our parents are just as worr, uh protective as you two," Grace said, swallowing the word *worry* just in time while pointing at Jory and Eric. Jory looked at Grace, letting her know he had noticed her slip. "I know that we are a pain in the ass right now, but we are parents, and that's what we're supposed to do, protecting you at all costs," said Jory, his tone full of understanding.

"Marcus, Gracie? Your father and I would appreciate it if you notify us before leaving the house. We didn't even know that you were gone. You could have been kidnapped, or worse," Max admonished.

"I'm sorry, mom, but we felt Chris' distress and needed to be with him asap," Grace explained. "What she said," Marcus chimed in, putting his arm around his sister's shoulder.

Jory motioned for Eric, James, and Max to follow him outside. "We need to give them some breathing space. Chris is fed up with being watched every minute of the day. He's an adult and needs his privacy. The same goes for Carmen, Marcus, and Grace. They are grownups now and combined; the four are powerful beyond any imagination," Eric softly said.

"Our children are connected; their bond is powerful. Just now, we got a small taste of it when Marcus and Grace felt Chris' distress. They immediately came to see him. I don't want to, but I think it's time to back off and let them deal with Dhidysus and Leldur. We will keep an eye on them in case they need our help; then, we will take action. Until then, we have to stand on the sideline, like it or not. I'm afraid that if we smother our children further, we will push them away," Jory said, eyeing James, Max, and Eric.

"I know you're right, but the need to protect is so strong," Max sighed. "I know, believe me, I know," Jory softly replied. James pulled Max close; he said, "We will back off, for now. We know it's not going to be easy, but what choice do we have?" They talked a bit longer and agreed to give the children more space.

The air moved, and Destiny appeared. She smiled and said, "This is how it's supposed to be. You need to trust that your children can defend themselves, and if they need help, they will ask. Trust each other; only then will the pack survive. If there's no trust, death and destruction will follow," she said. Then bright, sparkling light appeared, and Destiny was gone. *"Heed my warning, don't lose faith and trust each other."* Destiny's words echoed, and then all was quiet again like nothing had happened.

Max looked very confused, as did Eric and James. The alpha mate was the only one who seemed to understand what had happened; why Destiny had descended to earth? "They waited for us to decide to either back-off or smother the children. And when we think about it, if we had chosen the latter, we would probably have alienated our children from us. It's bad enough if something like that happened without the looming danger. Imagine driving a wedge between our children and us, with the danger we're facing," Jory said.

"Ah, now I understand. They needed us to make the decision without their involvement. It had to come from our hearts," said Max. "Exactly," the alpha mate smiled. "Still, I don't like it, and it won't get easy to let them go out there and take on Dhidysus and Leldur," the white tiger said. "Let's not forget Zachariah." Everyone looked at the sliding doors. "Grandfather," Jory said, looking intently at Dacian.

"I followed him for quite some time until the trail suddenly vanished. Strange, very strange. I've never experienced anything like this before," the archangel admitted. "What does that mean?" Jory questioned. "It means, my dear grandchild, that Dhidysus had help from a warlock. I looked closer at where the trail had ended, and it reeked of dark magic. It was overwhelming," Dacian replied.

"So, now we need to find out which warlock was foolish enough to aid Dhidysus." Jory, Eric, James, and Max, who still were outside, looked up at Chris. Behind him stood Carmen, Marcus, and Grace; all four looked grim. This was the first time Jory and Eric realized that their son and daughter were adults.

"Yes, you do," Jory said. Eric raised one eyebrow, eyeing his mate in question. "Remember what we talked about? We need to trust that they will ask for our help if they need it," Jory said. "Destiny warned us to trust each other, which means we need to share everything. So from now on, there will be no secrets between us. We share how we feel; we even share if we don't like the food. You know what I mean," Eric said. "I don't like it, but it's not that we have any other choice," said Max. "I agree," said James as he gently squeezed her shoulder.

"Then, I have a confession to make," Marcus said, looking uncertain. Grace moved until she was next to her brother and smiled encouragingly. "What is it, sweetheart?" Max questioned. Marcus looked from his parents to Eric and Jory. "You know that Chris had this vision of, well, murdering his dads?" Everyone nodded. "I had one that involved both of you," he added.

All eyes were on Marcus, then Max stood, walked to her son, and hugged him. "We believe in you and trust you. Your father and I know that you would never hurt us. It doesn't mean we dismiss this because it has to mean something," the white tiger said.

"Thank you for sharing, Marcus," a content-looking Eric said. "We heard Destiny's warning. I want the pack and our friends safe. So, if that means that I need to share my thoughts and fears, then so be it," Marcus said, but Eric could tell that the young man didn't feel comfortable, which was understandable.

"It will get challenging to have no secrets from each other, but when we go into battle, we need to trust each other blindly. I don't know why Destiny insisted on it, but I know that she has her reasons to warn us," Jory said. After that, they sat in silence for a long time until a car came up the driveway. "That would be Jack. I wonder what he wants?" Jory said and hoped that the jaguar was alright.

Eric walked inside and into the hall to let Jack in. "Hey Jack, not that I'm not happy to see you, but what brings you here?" the alpha inquired. "Beau is missing." It was now that Eric noticed that Jack was too pale, his eyes too hollow. Something was off, but Eric couldn't put his finger on it. He looked over his shoulder and called for his mate.

Jory's smile disappeared when he saw Jack standing in the doorway. He looked from Eric to Jack, and the alpha immediately felt Jory's unease. So, something was wrong; he was sure of it.

"Eric? Get away from him," Jory whispered. The alpha didn't need a second invitation and stepped back, or he tried. Before the alpha could respond, a fireball was thrown at him. However, Jory reacted faster, deflecting the demonic fireball and sending it right back to the demon who still had Jack's appearance. The demon tried to dodge the ball of fire but was too slow because he apparently hadn't expected that the damn thing would come back.

An explosion sounded as the demon got hit by his own ball of fire. Everyone rushed into the hall and came to a skidding halt staring at the scorch mark just outside.

Chapter Twelve

"What was that thing? And how did you know that it wasn't Jack?" James asked. It was a question they all wanted to be answered. "Don't forget I have the gift of seeing someone for who he really is. And, something felt off when he saw Jack. So, I gave him my 'special' look. That's when I saw the demon," the alpha mate explained.

He had the ability to see people for whom they really were. Plus, he could see a person's aura. "This particular demon didn't have an aura," Jory explained. Then the alpha mate looked thoughtful, frowned, and added. "Which was strange, now that I think about it. Even demons have an aura; they are mostly black, or something alike."

"Too bad we can't ask him what he was anymore because you vaporized him," Finn said. "I did, didn't I?" Jory chuckled. The moment the children were returned to the ranch after the aging process, Jory had gained a new power. He was now able to not only burn his enemies to ashes but could vaporize them on the spot.

They had gathered in the main house and were changing ideas on how to defend the ranch and its residents. Jory searched for and found his son and daughter, who were busy talking through the mind link they shared.

It troubled Jory that he wasn't able to listen in anymore because that could only mean that their children had shut them out on purpose. On the other hand, the alpha mate was glad that he still could see their auras, and they were a bright, almost blinding, silvery white. That meant that the four of them were pure of heart.

Suddenly, Dudley began to whine softly, but Jory could hear the fear in that barely audible sound. "People, Something bad is coming our way," he warned. "What is it, baby," Eric asked, and Jory could see that his mate was on high alert, just like the rest.

Jory pointed to Dudley, who still was softly whining, only now Molly, Sage, and Chloe were joining in. Chris and Carmen, as well as

Marcus and Grace, rose and moved to the sliding doors that led to the back deck.

When Eric and Jory wanted to enter the back deck to see why the children had gone to the deck, Carmen motioned for them to stay inside. *"Stay inside, all of you, please? Daddy, I need to concentrate on the danger, and I need to know that you are safe, all of you,"* Carmen's whisper flowed through Jory's mind like a warm summer breeze. Oh, how he had missed that.

The alpha mate used the mind link between him and Eric and let the alpha know what Carmen had told him. Eric looked at the people standing behind him, ready to defend; he didn't say anything but held his hand up. Everyone knew what that meant and that, later on, Eric would explain. So, for now, everyone had to stay inside.

Eric and Jory eyed each other, and both silently agreed that this was probably the most challenging thing they had ever done. Because they had to step aside to let their kids, their adult children, handle the situation.

Chris, Carmen, Marcus, and Grace stood next to each other on the back deck, holding hands. Jory was wondering what the children saw that they didn't, when dark clouds were coming their way. The alpha noticed that the wind was picking up.

The clouds were slowly heading toward the ranch, and it was getting dark outside. "Shit, even the night isn't as dark as this," Jory whispered. Eric didn't reply but gently squeezed his mate's shoulder.

Jory gasped when he saw Carmen glow. At first, it was a gentle, soft glow, but it got steadily brighter and brighter. She was shining like a beacon in the night. It was an eerie sight, but no one was afraid; if anything, they were in awe of Carmen's appearance.

Jory had no words to describe his daughter at that moment because nothing would do. The alpha mate also saw that Chris, Marcus, and Grace had moved until they were standing behind Carmen. Chris on her left, touching her left shoulder. Grace stood in the middle touching

Carmen between her shoulder blades. Marcus was to her right, touching Carmen's right shoulder.

The wind had turned into a storm, and it was all Eric, Jory, James, and Max could do not to open the sliding doors and rush outside to defend their children. This was the time to let go. However, at the slightest sign that the children were in over their heads, Eric, Jory, James, and Max would be at their side.

At first, Jory wondered what they were doing, but then it clicked. The children stayed connected because it gave Carmen more power. It was evident that Carmen was playing the leading part.

Eric took Jory's hand, and together they stood behind the now closed sliding doors, watching the children do their thing. The alpha mate knew his kids were powerful, but it was hard to stand back and do nothing.

Even though Carmen shone very bright, they couldn't see around her because the rest of the back deck and the garden were cloaked in darkness. Nevertheless, it was obvious that this wasn't a typical storm, and everyone was watching as Carmen spread her arms, lifted her head, and began to chant.

The alpha and his mate continued to watch through the front of the sliding doors, James and Max at their side. The rest of the pack and the angels, archangel, the God of War, and the witches stood behind them. Everyone watched in awe when Carmen's power manifested itself for the first time. Even though Carmen hadn't used her power before, she seemed to know exactly what to do and how to control it.

"I can't believe what I'm seeing," Jory whispered in awe. Carmen was chanting louder now, and the powerful wind she unleashed was becoming visible. It was a pure white, with streaks of several colors of blue. It was a sight for sore eyes if the situation hadn't been so dire.

The storm Carmen unleashed stayed put; it didn't move toward the deadly storm that was coming their way. Jory frowned because he didn't understand why Carmen didn't push her wind force forward to destroy the storm that was evidently caused by black magic.

Then he got his answer why Carmen kept her storm on the leash. The alpha mate heard Chris, Marcus, and Grace chanting now as well. "Look," Eric whispered. The storm Carmen had conjured was clearly visible, and they watched in astonishment as the clouds joined the wind. Jory heard Jake gasp as the storm and clouds mixed and formed a giant ball.

All four were chanting louder and louder until Carmen moved her arm, stretching them in front of her, sending the storm toward the dark storm that was frighteningly close now. So close that they felt the house shake. The bright white storm, which now had dark blue streaks in it, clashed with the all-consuming, black as night storm. The collision caused a blinding orb, then it was over, and the sun was, once again, shining.

All four children turned simultaneously, and Jory was shocked to see Carmen's pale face. He wanted to open the sliding doors and rush outside to check on his daughter, but something held him back. Carmen stayed where she was flanked by Marcus and Grace while Chris walked up to the sliding doors. He didn't enter the room, however, but instead requested water for all four.

"Sure, but I need to know, are all of you alright?" the alpha asked, concern evident in his voice. Chris looked tired, but he assured his dads that they were fine, tired but fine. Even though Jory had wanted to see for himself that the children were alright, he nodded, turned, and went into the kitchen to get four bottles of water.

"What the hell did we witness just now?" James growled. He was moving passed Eric and Jory and would have opened the sliding doors if Eric hadn't held him back. "They need some time to collect themselves," the alpha softly explained. James nodded, and Jory and Eric could tell that the sheriff wasn't happy. "It's so new for all of us, including our children," Jory said. "We know, but I still want to go out there and hug my boy and my girl. Need to see for myself if they are alright," Max softly replied. "Join the club," the alpha mumbled.

Chapter Thirteen

"I still can't believe that our little girl is so powerful. I thought that only Chris had gained special powers, but it seemed that Carmen got some too," Jory said while mixing the salad. They were busy cooking dinner while James and Eric were checking the horses. "I wonder if Marcus and Grace got them too," Max said as she continued chopping tomatoes and onions.

"We gave all four children special powers," said a voice behind them, making Jory smile and Max jump. It was late in the afternoon, and Chris explained how he, Marcus, and Grace had amplified Carmen's powers by touching her. Everyone had been impressed because no one had ever witnessed that much power being released, not even by Eric or Jory.

"Gaia? Welcome," Jory said, smiling. "Hello," Max greeted politely. The alpha mate could tell that she still felt uneasy in the presence of Gaia. Well, who wouldn't? After all, Mother Earth was a pretty powerful lady.

"I'm not here to tell you which powers we granted the four because that's something they need to experience themselves before they can explain it to you," Gaia said. She eyed them, closed her eyes, and the next moment Eric and James stepped into the kitchen.

"Thank you," said Gaia because she was the one who had summoned them. "What I have to say concerns you and the ranch's residents." She looked at James and Max, then said, "You will move to the ranch until the danger has passed." "So, we are in danger as well?" James questioned. Gaia nodded. "Yes, you are. But, the real reason I want you here is that the four need to stay together if you want to survive," Gaia spoke softly, but the tone in which she spoke was loud and clear. Do as I say, and live. Defy me, and you probably will die.

James eyed his mate; he said, "Well, we better go home and start packing." "Not on your own because it's too dangerous. Take the four;

they should be able to protect you," Mother Earth urged. "We're ready when you are," Grace said. Max looked up and was stunned that her daughter appeared calm, almost serene.

"Aren't you worried that someone will attack us on our way home?" Max questioned. If it was up to her, then Grace was still her little girl. Even though they had many memories of their children growing up, it was still very strange.

"No, as long as the four of us are together, we should practically be unbeatable," Grace said matter of factly. Max pressed her lips together, and for a moment, Jory thought she would protest and tell everyone that she was their children's protector and not the other way around. However, Max rose and pulled James with her. "Alright, let's go home and pack," she said. Then she eyed Jory and added, "You really don't mind?" "Do I need to kick your ass?" the alpha mate chuckled. "No, I'm thrilled to have you all here with us. That way, I know that you're safe," Jory added.

"Let Finn and Felicia take you," Gaia urged. "I can take you," Felicia said. "I'll accompany you anyway," Finn chimed in. "Ah, you think I'm incapable of orbing six people at once?" Felicia said. "I certainly do," Finn teased. They all knew that Finn had never doubted Felicia, and he wasn't doing it now.

"So, you take five persons, and I'll take one?" Felicia chuckled. "No, no, we both take three," Finn smiled; he loved to banter with Felicia. "No, Finn, you take the four," Gaia insisted. Then, she looked at Felicia, "you take James and Max because I don't want the four separated," Mother Earth explained.

"We can orb; all of us have that ability," Chris said, looking confused because why let Finn and Felicia take them when it wasn't necessary? "I want you safe, and the best way to do that is to let Finn orb you to the Stanton Residence," Gaia said. "Are you telling us that it's not safe for us to orb right now?" Marcus questioned.

"Precisely. If you orb, it leaves a trail. And we don't want Zachariah, Dhidysus, and Leldur to know that you left the ranch because it could trigger an unexpected attack." Gaia paused, then added, in a whisper, "I'm not sure if everyone would survive."

Chris looked alarmed. "What if they are watching the ranch? Wouldn't they know we left, even if Finn orbed us out?" Chris asked because he didn't like the idea of a surprise attack. He knew how powerful Zachariah was, so if he had the aid of Dhidysus and Leldur, who knew what they were capable of?

"You need to protect James and Max, and the only way to do that is to stay together, as the four," Gaia said, and her tone let Chris know it was final. He eyed Gaia, then said, "I hope that nothing happens while we're away." Gaia didn't answer; instead, she said, "Go, and hurry back." So Finn took the four, and Felicia took James and Max. Bright lights surrounded them; then they were gone.

James and Max immediately started packing clothes and things they would need for their stay at the ranch. "Mom, dad, we really need to go now," Grace urged. Max, who was busy putting her e-reader in her bag, looked up. "Is something the matter? We're not even ten minutes gone," she said, sounding worried. "Just hurry, okay, mom?" Grace insisted. "Alright, I'm ready," Max said. "Me too," James said. "Then let's go," Grace urged.

They were back at the ranch in the blink of an eye. "That was fast," Dorian said. "Yes, we don't need that much, and the things I forgot, you guys will provide," the white tiger replied. "We will," said Jory. "Let me show you your room," the alpha mate passed James and Max and headed for the stairs. "Dorian was right; that was really quick," he frowned.

"Yeah, well, Grace insisted that we needed to leave as soon as possible," James replied. "That's not good." The alpha mate barely had finished his sentence when all hell broke loose. A loud bang shook the house, making James, Max, and Jory rush back to the living room.

"Oh holy hell," the alpha mate cursed when he looked out the window and saw Zachariah standing in the garden. Before anyone could react, the four opened the sliding doors and rushed onto the deck. "Oh dear God," Max whispered when she saw Zachariah standing in the garden. The monster was over seven feet tall and had deadly, razor-sharp claws.

It was evident that Zachariah hadn't known that the four were adults now because, for a moment, his eyes grew big and showed fear and uncertainty. He covered quickly, though.

"You have quite some power, little girl," Zachariah taunted. "So you noticed, uh? And as you can see, we are not so little anymore. Chris could defend himself against you when he was just a toddler. Do you really think you could defeat him now?" Grace replied, her tone taunting, and Max was shocked at how cold her daughter's tone was. "Oh, I noticed the ripple of power, and I'm sure the rest of the universe did too when the storm I had sent to destroy the ranch and everyone in it was neutralized. So, that was you, little girl." Zachariah's tone sounded more threatening now.

"Yes, that was little Ol' me," Grace said in a too calm voice. "Ah, I will destroy all of you because to me, you're still children." "Yeah, well, we will kill anyone who tries to harm us. So, listen carefully because I won't repeat, and you won't get a second chance," Grace paused, then added, "If you leave now and never return, we will let you live. But, stay and attack us, and we will kill you."

James put his arm around his mate's shoulder in silent comfort. "I don't like this one bit," she whispered. "None of us do, Max. But we need to let them do their thing. Gaia said they are ready, and we have to trust her," Jory whispered. Their eyes locked on their children, who were holding hands.

Suddenly Zachariah raised his arms, and the air began to move, like a wave, and it was heading for the four, who stood their ground. Then they let go of their hands, and Chris raised his hands to ward off whatever was coming their way. After about a minute, Carmen, Grace, and Marcus followed Chris' lead, and together they sent the airwave back toward Zachariah.

"What are you doing? This shouldn't be possible," Zachariah growled as the superwave hit him full force. He tumbled back but gained ground immediately. "Now you really pissed me off," he growled while conjuring what looked like four giant dogs but ten times more deadly.

"Shit, hellhounds," Jory whispered from behind the sliding doors. Eric grabbed his arm when Jory was about to open the doors. "No, baby. We need to let them defend the ranch. Remember that we promised Gaia we wouldn't intervene," the alpha whispered. Jory didn't like it but knew that Eric was right. He hated every single moment their children were outside facing one of the deadliest monsters.

Zachariah's grin was one of pure evil when he commanded the hounds to attack the four. To everyone's astonishment and horror, all four hounds went straight for Chris. "Enough," Jory said as he began to glow. "NO," Eric commanded. The alpha used his power as true alpha to keep his mate from going outside and joining the fight.

"Let me go," Jory growled. "No, I'm sorry, baby, but I can't allow you to interfere. We need to trust our children; they can hold their own. Look," Eric said as Chris grabbed the first hellhound by the throat, lifted him, and threw him against a tree. In the meantime, Marcus had seized the second one and crushed the animal's throat, then to be sure the hound was dead; he broke its neck as well.

Carmen was facing the third giant hound, and it looked like she didn't know how to kill it. Chris was at her side in seconds and snapped its neck. Grace didn't get the chance to fight the last hound because Marcus reacted fast; he took the hound and sliced open its throat. While Marcus was ending the third hound's life, the one who was thrown against a tree by Chris attacked Grace.

It happened so fast that Marcus couldn't react in time. Chris, however, could and caught the beast in mid-jump and ripped his throat open. The hound fell to the ground and didn't move anymore. Zachariah wasn't grinning anymore. "I will be back, and then I'll destroy each and every one of you," he growled. He was about to disappear when Chris pointed both hands at him, and a streak of blueish fire hit Zachariah right in the chest. The monster seemed to hover for a moment, roared in pain, then he was gone.

Chapter Fourteen

Everyone talked simultaneously but quieted down when the four entered the house. Max rushed to Marcus and Grace and hugged the life out of them. Jory did the same with Chris and Carmen.

"Are you alright?" Jory asked while checking his son and daughter for injuries. "We're fine, dad," Carmen assured. "No, you're not," said Sarah as she lifted Chris' shirt, and a deep laceration became visible. "Oh hell," Jory looked horrified because the wound was deep. "Let me take care of that," Sarah said as she left to get the first aid kit.

"That was done by one of the hellhounds, right?" Eric questioned. "Yep, the bastard managed to slice my side before I threw him against the tree," Chris replied. Sarah returned and eyed Eric, and the alpha saw the worried expression on her face.

"Is it that bad?" he asked. She nodded, "I'm afraid so. Well, at least with normal shifters. Since Chris isn't a regular shifter, I don't know if, or how it will manifest," she eyed Chris. "We need to." Well, all be damned," cursed a stunned Sarah when she saw the wound heal before her eyes.

"How?" "I'm just as stunned as you are," said Chris, and he was because he didn't know that his body had the ability to heal itself. "It's reassuring that you heal yourself," said Jory. "Still, it's odd that I didn't know," Chris insisted. "Well, I think it's a good thing," Eric said.

The alpha mate looked over at his best friend. Max still looked shaken, probably because she was a mother now. Max had never been scared, but now, she was afraid for the safety of her children. She held Marcus by the shoulders. "Don't ever scare me like that again," a trembling Max admonished. Then she hugged both children again.

"That was scary as hell," Emma chimed in while Ares protectively slid his arm around her waist. The God of War hadn't said anything during Zachariah's attack. He had, however, kept Emma safely in his arms.

"I wonder if Zachariah will come back now that he knows that Chris is an adult," Jake said. The young shifter had joined the pack after he was forced to attack the Wentworth Pack, which he had refused. Instead, he'd let them capture him. He was now a member of Eric's pack.

Chris' smile was rueful; he said, "I'm afraid we haven't seen the last of him. Plus, he now knows that I'm an adult. So, it's a matter of time before Dhidysus and Leldur know it too. Unfortunately, is our advantage gone too."

Eric cocked his head, listening. "The barn. Something is happening at the barn," the alpha said as he ran outside, where he abruptly came to a stop. A dozen hellhounds blocked the path to the barn, where the horses screamed in fear.

"Beau," Chris whispered as he stormed after his father, he was followed by the rest. Carmen, Marcus, and Grace rushed past the others, and they, too, came to a screeching halt at seeing a dozen hellhounds.

"What the fuck?" Chris growled; he was getting angrier by the second when he heard the horses scream and stomp their hoofs, trying to escape the danger. Max was the first one who changed into her tiger, as she immediately charged the hounds. Max was attacked by four of the beasts, and that was when it all went to hell.

Marcus and Grace rushed to their mother's aid. Marcus grabbed one of the hounds who were clawing at Max's back, slicing her open. Suddenly everything around Marcus went quiet. One look told Marcus that he was alone, his mother severely wounded. "What the hell?" he growled as he began to call for the others.

"Chris, Carmen, Grace? Where are you? Eric, Jory, help, please? Mother is dying if she doesn't get treatment. Please please, help. God damn, where is everyone?" Marcus growled in desperation as tears began to fall.

He leaned toward Max, but the white tiger lay motionless on the sandy ground. "Mom, please, open your eyes. I'll get us help, but you need to hold on," Marcus mumbled while he carefully put Max's head in his lap. "No no no," he cried when Max's breathing was getting more difficult by the minute. Then, her breathing slowed and finally stopped altogether.

Marcus lifted his head and screamed his rage to the heavens. "You promised that she wouldn't be harmed. You promised! Now my mother is dead. You broke your promise; now I will brake mine," he growled in a voice that was barely sounding human.

Marcus didn't know how long he had been sitting at his mother's side, hoping that he was wrong or that Gaia would bring her back. However, nothing happened, as it was getting dark.

Sitting next to his mother's dead body had calmed Marcus somewhat. It was now that he took in his surroundings and noticed that he wasn't at the ranch anymore. "What the fuck is going on? Where am I?" he whispered.

The death of his mother had made Marcus lose focus on everything else. Now that he had calmed down, his thoughts became rational again. Was this real? Someone had managed to mess with his mind during his aging. Was it possible that this same person had managed to do it once again?

Marcus lifted his head and looked at the sky, or what was supposed to be the sky, but it was purple. Everywhere Marcus looked, he saw, well, nothing. No trees, no bushes. The vast expanse consisted only of sand and nothing else. It felt like he was in the wastelands. Then it dawned on him.

"Oh, shit. None of this is real, isn't it?" Marcus said in a firm voice that showed he had no doubts. Marcus glared at the body of his supposedly deceased mother and saw that she slowly was dissolving until she vanished altogether. Then Marcus saw the ranch reappear, and the pack, the angels, archangel, and even Ares were staring at him.

"Where did you go? Shit, we thought that Zachariah got to you," Chris said as he hugged his best friend. "Marcus? Son, are you alright? What happened?" James asked while Max stood behind her mate, looking strangely at her son.

The white tiger was pale and looked exhausted, but she was alive because this was the here and now; this was real. "I'm alright, Marcus. I didn't die," Max whispered before she flung herself to Marcus. Mother and son were holding each other tightly. "I'm so sorry, so sorry," Max kept repeating. Eric wanted to know what was going on between Max and Marcus, but before he could say anything, the hellhounds attacked once again.

"Those damn beasts keep coming, and their numbers are growing," Jory growled, then he glanced at the four and nodded. "Show us what you can, how powerful you are," the alpha mate said. The four smiled evilly as they spread out and systematically began to kill the hounds. Jory was sure that the children were telepathically communicating with each other. Because only then could they work efficiently.

However, more and more hellhounds appeared, and Chris reached out to Jory, asking him to join the fight. The alpha mate and the rest were eager to kill those damn beasts, and it didn't take long before everyone was fighting. Jory estimated that about fifty hounds were attacking the ranch. So, yes, everyone was eager to join the fight and tear those godforsaken beasts' heads from the torsos.

Marcus' nightmare came to life when Max was attacked by four hounds, who seemed to work together. Max would be able to take one, maybe two down. But Grace was fast and grabbed a hellhound, shook the damn beast, and slammed it against the wooden fence. "NO, not again," Marcus screamed in rage as he called on his fire and burned two. Max growled when her son wanted to get the fourth hound because she wanted to kill it. Her tiger needed the kill, and it was ferocious, tearing the hellhound apart.

Jory unleashed his blueish but very deadly fire and took one beast down. Jake had offered to get to the barn and keep the horses safe. Emma had rushed after Jake, and of course, Ares ran after Emma. JJ and Armand followed suit because they didn't know if and how many hellhounds were in the barn.

It turned out that five more hellhounds were in the barn, terrifying the horses to the limit. Chris wanted to go into the barn to destroy the beasts, but he was needed outside, where more hellhounds appeared. "This is madness," said James as he caught one of the beasts and broke its neck. "It seems that more and more are coming. We can't hold them off for long," Dorian growled as he grabbed a hound and tore its throat out.

When Chris heard Beau scream in agony, it was more than he could take. He stopped fighting and raised his arms to the heavens, making the earth shake. "ENOUGH!" he roared. The hounds whined and retreated, the horses seemed to quiet down, and they saw the beasts vanish.

"You couldn't do that right away?" Marcus chuckled. With a crooked smile, Chris said, "Of course, I could, but then we would have missed all the fun." "I killed two of them," Carmen stated proudly. "Only one," Grace said. "I slaughtered six of the fuckers," Chris growled. "Three," Marcus chimed in.

"What?" Chris said when he saw everyone staring at them. "Weren't you afraid of those beasts?" Emma asked in disbelief. The four shook their heads because they really hadn't been afraid.

Chris eyed his fathers. "Can we talk? I need to tell you something, and no, it's not bad. In fact, it's good news, very good news," he said, smiling. Eric and Jory nodded, excused themselves, and followed Chris, who headed for Jory's study.

They sat down and eyed their son with curiosity. "So, what is it you want to talk to us about?" the alpha mate began. Chris grinned. "I have a girlfriend," he stated and held his hand up when Jory opened his mouth to say something. "It's all very new. I met her two weeks ago in town when I was buying groceries."

"How wonderful, how does she look? How old is she? What's her name?" Jory fired question after question. "Calm down, and let the man explain," Eric chuckled as he wrapped his arms around his mate. "Her name is Alyssa Knight, and she moved recently to Willows Creek. She is a human and works at the coffee shop.

"When do we meet her," Jory asked. "Soon, we just need to spend more time together before I introduce her to the pack. And remember, she's human," Chris said, looking from Eric to Jory. He knew that his dads wouldn't mind if he brought a human girlfriend home, but still, he was a bit nervous about their reaction because of all that was going on.

"Alright, son, let us know when you're ready to bring her to the ranch," Eric said, smiling. "Is she *the one*?" Chris pressed his lips together. "I believe so, yes," he softly replied. "Oh, that would be so wonderful," Jory cooed as he hugged his son. "Whoa, easy, dad. I'm still not entirely sure," Chris cautioned. "You will meet her soon; however, I do have one request." "Shoot," the alpha mate said, still grinning. "Let's keep it between us for now. Only Carmen, Marcus, and Grace know about it. But it's not as if I can keep anything from them," he chuckled. "Of course," Eric and Jory replied in unison.

Chapter Fifteen

"Do you have any idea of who could have that much power to mess with your mind? Because this shouldn't be possible," Chris said. Ever since they were kids, Chris, Carmen, Marcus, and Grace had managed to prevent anyone from entering their minds. So, that it had happened now, and to Chris as well, didn't sit well with the four.

Marcus shook his head. "Not a clue. But I want your promise that if we find out who did this to me, that bastard is mine. No one but me touches him," he said, his voice dark with rage. "You have my word," Chris assured his friend.

"I can only imagine the hell you went through watching your mother die. We will find out who it was, and that person will have to answer to you," Chris said in a firm tone. He, too, was furious. "It also means that we all have to be even more careful than before," Eric replied, and he was glad that most of his horses had been sold. Roman, the stallion who had gotten Daisy pregnant, and of course Daisy, Beau, Skyler, and Happy, JJ's horse, were the only ones left. Eric had decided they wouldn't breed horses until the danger was over.

Marcus had explained what had happened, and then, to everyone's astonishment, Max shared what had happened to her. It turned out that someone let her see what Marcus went through—seeing his mother die and not being able to help her. Max had seen and felt everything that her son had been going through.

Billy and Evan returned from checking on the horses, and Eric was relieved to hear they were okay. The horses still were skittish, but other than that, they were fine. Emma was in the kitchen preparing dinner, Ares by her side, when she felt dizzy. "What's wrong, honey?" A worried Ares asked as he pulled back a chair so Emma could sit down.

"I. I don't know. I was just a bit dizzy, but I'm fine now," she replied. "You need to let the doctor examine you. With all that's going on, who knows," Ares insisted. Emma conceded, but only so Ares would feel better. God, the man, was protective as hell.

Cassandra entered the kitchen because she wanted to help Emma cooking dinner. However, the witch turned and hurried to the living room, with Emma and Ares hot on her heels. When they stepped into the room, Eric cocked his head; the alpha was listening. A moment later, Damian materialized in the middle of the room.

Eric immediately knew that something must be very wrong because the master vampire would never intrude like he had done now if it wasn't urgent. Eric eyed Damian. "We need help. The coven is under attack. They have Shawn; they captured my beloved. The coven is fighting like hell right this moment," Damian growled.

"Do you know who is attacking the coven?" Jory questioned because if they went in, it wouldn't be with their eyes closed. "Zachariah, and Leldur. They have hellhounds doing their bidding. We need to hurry," the master vampire urged.

Chris eyed Carmen, Marcus, and Grace, who nodded. "Alright, let's kick ass and get Shawn back," Chris said. "All of us will help, all but Evan and Billy; I want you to stay here at the ranch, just in case," Eric said. Both men nodded, then the angels and Dacian orbed part of the pack, and Damian, took Eric and Jory. They wanted to take the four, but Chris touched Marcus, Carmen, and Grace, then he disappeared. Jory, Eric, James, and Max didn't have time to react because a moment later, they stood in what seemed like a big house. The noise they heard let them know where the fight was. They rushed outside and jumped into the fray.

"Ah, there you are again, little girl," Zachariah taunted as he saw Grace take down one of the hounds. "Screw you, monster," Grace yelled as she lunged at him. That was what Zachariah had been waiting for. "NO," Marcus yelled when Zachariah grinned evilly and grabbed Grace by the throat. Marcus and Carmen changed their focus from the hellhounds to Zachariah, who became their target.

Carmen raised her hands, making it storm, but only around Zachariah. "Damn, she's good," Chris whispered as he saw his sister controlling the wind. Carmen began to swirl her hands, and the storm wrapped around Zachariah, who didn't laugh anymore. Carmen kept tightening the storm around the monster, intending to crush his lungs.

Could he actually die? Carmen wasn't sure, but she could at least try it. Zachariah began to scream and was fighting the storm that wrapped tighter and tighter around his massive body.

Leldur, who saw Zachariah gasping for air, was about to disappear when Eric grabbed him. "Oh no, not so fast. Where is Shawn?" the alpha demanded. "I don't know what you're talking about," the fallen God answered. "Listen, you idiot, don't let me repeat myself," Eric's growl was deep and menacing.

When Leldur still refused to talk, Eric had enough because he didn't have time to make this idiot see the error of his ways. Eric tightened his grip, and then the true alpha unleashed his power. If Leldur thought he was untouchable, the fallen God was badly mistaken because he, too, needed to breathe.

The alpha hadn't even noticed that the fighting had stopped, and the hellhounds had disappeared. The entire coven was watching Carmen dealing with Zachariah. Eric was joined by Jory, and together, they were squeezing the information, about Shawn's whereabouts, out of Leldur. Marcus and Chris were guarding their surroundings and would kill anyone who tried to attack them.

"Oh hell, what are you doing? This. This shouldn't be possible," Leldur croaked when it became difficult to breathe. The fallen God couldn't be killed easily, but Eric could torture him by depriving him of oxygen.

"Where is Shawn," Eric repeated. "May I?" the alpha mate calmly asked his mate. Jory, who had befriended Shawn, wouldn't be so patient with Leldur. Eric nodded, "Of course, baby. Give it your best shot," he grinned evilly. Jory raised his arms and pointed at the fallen God. "You fire can't kill me," Leldus said, but he didn't look convinced. "That's right, it can't, but it can hurt you and make you wish you were dead," Jory growled as he sent the deadly blueish fire straight into Leldur's chest, making him scream in agony.

"Stop, make it stop," he screamed. But, Jory didn't stop; instead, he pushed more power into the fire. Leldur roared in pain, and was that fear in his eyes. Jory thought so, well, good. "This is your last chance to tell us where Shawn is held captive. If you refuse, then I will rain down on you like the hammer of Thor," Jory said in a too calm tone.

"Believe me when I say that you don't want to anger the alpha mate any further," Chris growled menacingly. "Alright, alright, I'll tell you where they took him," Leldur screamed. "Hades has him." That was all Leldus was able to say. "No, you fucking traitor. Hades will have your head for your betrayal," Zachariah roared as he forgot all about Grace, who had been distracted by Leldus' torture. Her hold on Zachariah had lessened, and he threw her aside like she weighed nothing and lunged for Leldur. Jory and Eric didn't even try to stop Zachariah when he grabbed Leldur and disappeared.

Damian was beside himself, and Eric and Jory understood. The master vampire was granted only one beloved; Shawn was it for Damian. He was deeply in love with his beloved. Darius MacCallan, Damian's brother, came to stand beside Eric and Jory.

"As you surely understand, we need to get Shawn back, or my brother won't survive. He will go insane to the point that we need to put him down, and that's not an option," Darius said. "So, can we count on you?" he softly added. "Absolutely," Eric answered without hesitation.

"How do we get to the underworld? We need to hurry because before Hades moves Shawn to another place," Jory insisted. "I know how we get there," Grace said. Jory wanted to ask how she knew but decided against it because now was not the time.

"We need Ares to bring us; he's the God of War and should be able to enter the underworld," Grace said matter of factly. "Of course, why didn't I think of that," Jory chuckled. The alpha mate called Ares and the God materialized in front of them a minute later. "What is it that you need?" Ares addressed Jory, not Eric. Somehow the alpha and the God of War didn't like each other. Maybe it was the fact that Eric's sister, Emma, was Ares' mate? Probably.

"Is it true that you can access the underworld?" Jory questioned. The alpha mate was well aware that Ares could, but he needed to hear it from the man himself. Plus, he wanted to see if Ares would be truthful. The God of War looked surprised. "I can," he admitted without hesitation. "Then you need to take us there because we need to rescue Shawn, Damian's beloved," the alpha mate explained curtly.

Ares raised one eyebrow. "Do you have any idea of how dangerous that place is? And what makes you think that Shawn is there any way?" Ares questioned. "We squeezed it out of Leldur before a furious Zachariah took him to God knows where." This time it was Chris who replied.

"Before we go, there are a few things that you need to know," Ares, who still had his arm around Emma, gently squeezed her shoulder before pulling back. "Then hurry because we don't know how much time Shawn has in the clutches of that maniac," Chris said, looking straight at Ares.

The God of War nodded in approval. "You have balls, Chris; I like it," Ares' grin was evil but not hostile. "Once you're there, there's no telling if you can still use magic, special powers, or whatever. That place is unpredictable, and to make it worse, Hades rules it," Ares paused.

"Yeah, well, it's not like we have a choice. We need to get Shawn back, and Eric, the children, and I will do what's necessary to achieve that," Jory insisted. "Yep, and soon because Damian is a mess, and we want to leave before he decides to come with us," Chris said.

Chapter Sixteen

"Sweet Jesus, what is this place," Jory whispered as he took in his surroundings. Eric, Jory, and the four stood in the middle of, well, nothing. They were surrounded by darkness but still were able to see each other, which was strange.

Ares lifted his head; he was listening. "Damn, Hades must already know we're here because I can hear his dog," the God of War whispered as he drew his sword. "Dog? I hear several dogs barking," Eric said. "This particular one has two heads and razor-sharp teeth," Ares informed them.

Then the huge monster Hades called a dog came into sight. "Sweet hell, he's huge," Jory whispered. "Kill it, and it will tick Hades off for sure," Ares chuckled. "Nice," Marcus said. The four took their positions, as did Eric and Jory, and of course, Ares.

"Let me have him," Ares growled. The God of War didn't wait for an answer but charged as soon as the beast approached. The children, Eric and Jory watched as Ares, with one swift move, beheaded one of the heads of the monster dog. "Oh shit, look," Chris said as he pointed at the dog whose head was growing back.

"Now, you may help me," Ares grinned. And, it was obvious, by the way, he was acting, that he had a history with the beast. Chris and Marcus went for the left head and Carmen, Grace, and Ares for the other one.

Eric and Jory eyed each other; the alpha mockingly said, "Tell me again why we came along?" "Your guess is as good as mine," the alpha mate chuckled but never took his eyes off the fight in front of them.

Grace had drawn a sword from what appeared out of nowhere and was slicing the beast's open, making it roar in a fury. Carmen and Ares stood side by side. She had stabbed the beast in its left eye while Ares concentrated on the beast's throat.

"Shit, do you see that?" Jory said in disbelief when the left eye Carmen had stabbed healed itself. "What is that monster?" Eric whispered.

A voice from behind them answered that question. "That's my dog, and it can't be defeated," Hades said as he grabbed Jory and disappeared. It happened so fast that Eric needed a second to comprehend what had happened.

"NO! Jory," the alpha screamed in rage. The huge dog vanished, leaving the others stunned. "Damn, the bastard did this just so he could get his claws into Jory," Ares growled, and now the God of War sounded pissed off. Ares knew how fond Emma was of her brother and Jory; she adored him. So, that the alpha mate had been taken by Hades of all people made the rage in Ares surface.

"Where is his lair? Because I'm going to rip the bastard to pieces," Eric's voice was barely human, as his eyes began to glow. It wouldn't take long until the true alpha would show, and if that happened, then God help them all.

Eric had two werewolf forms, a four-legged and a two-legged one, and he had unleashed great power when it became necessary. However, no one had ever seen the real true alpha. It had been predicted that Eric was a mighty creature. But would he be able to take on Hades?

"So, it seems that all of you managed to keep control of your magic after all. That's good because we will need every ounce of it to get Jory and Shawn back," a grim-looking Ares said.

"Bring us to his lair," Eric growled. "You can do that yourself. Just think of it, and you will get there," the God of War explained. Eric vanished within a second; he was followed by the four children and Ares.

Jory scanned the room he was in. It had happened so fast that it took the alpha mate a few seconds to understand what had happened. When he knew Hades had taken him, Jory raised his hands to unleash his deadly blueish fire. However, his arms didn't listen, and nothing happened. He tried again, but still nothing. "What did you do to me?" Jory growled.

Hades grinned evilly when he said, "I tied your hands, as simple as that." "Where's Shawn?" the alpha mate asked; by asking questions, he could stall because he needed time to think. Plus, he really wanted to know where Damian's mate was. Jory prayed that the man was still alive.

"He's alive, for now," Hades replied to Jory's unspoken question. "Why him?" the alpha mate continued questioning Hades. Hades' expression turned grim. "That's none of your business," he growled. Jory frowned because was Hades pissed off about that last question? It sure looked like it.

Alright, time for another question. "Why do you hate my pack so much?" Jory asked, his eyes never wavering; he kept staring into Hades' black as coal eyes. The ruler of the underworld considered Jory for a long time. "That's none of your business," he finally answered.

"That's where you're wrong. The pack is my family, so yes, it's my business," the alpha mate state. "Let me ask you a question." "What is Shawn to you? He's the coven leader's beloved. You're the mate of Eric Wentworth," Hades spat out Eric's name like he had dirt in his mouth.

Jory frowned, so Hades seemed to hate Eric; the question now was, why? Had Hades taken him because of Eric? The pack and especially Eric and Jory, were close with Damian's coven. Was he so stupid to enrage a true alpha? Even though Jory had never seen Eric using his full power, he instinctively knew that his mate was very powerful. He was curious as to what Eric really was capable of.

"Are you working with Zachariah, Dhidysus, and Leldur?" Jory asked. Because even though it didn't seem likely, one never knew. "No, why would I get involved with Dhidysus and Leldur? They are stupid as fuck. Now, Zachariah, well, he's a different story," Hades admitted, and it looked like he wanted to say more, but he didn't.

Of course, Jory's curiosity was aroused. "Why is Zachariah different?" Hades lifted his head, and Jory knew that he was listening. Then, the God of the Underworld eyed the alpha mate. "That's a story for another time," he said as he waved his hand, and in the blink of an eye, Jory was transported to another room. "What the fuck?" he growled. The room was nice enough, with a comfortable-looking couch and two matching chairs, a coffee table, and even a huge TV.

Was he in Hades' private quarters? Surely not. Jory concentrated on Eric and their two children. Maybe, just maybe, he could let them know where he was. The alpha mate closed his eyes and focussed on his mate and children with all his might, hoping they felt him reaching out.

"Dad?" Eric and Carmen turned and eyed Chris in confusion. "Didn't you feel that?" Chris said, looking aghast. "What are you talking about?" Carmen asked. "I felt, dad, reaching out to us," Chris insisted. Ares frowned and gave Chris a look that clearly said he thought he had lost his mind.

"You said that on the astral plane, many things are possible." "I know what I said, but we're not in Kansas anymore. Even though we're on the astral plane, we are, in fact, in the underworld. The underworld is part of the astral plane. So, when we went after Hades, we landed on his turf," Ares interrupted. "Oh hell," Eric cursed. "Well said," Ares agreed.

"So, this is the underworld," Chris said; it wasn't a question. During their aging process, Gaia and Chaos had fed them every information about the underworld that was known to them. But, Gaia and even Chaos didn't know every detail about the underworld simply because, after creating the place, they had left Hades to it.

"Alright, we need to find Hades' lair and kick his ass," Marcus growled. "Agreed," Carmen and Grace said simultaneously. Then, suddenly, their surroundings changed, and they found themselves in a room with, well, Hades.

"Welcome," the ruler of the underworld greeted. "Where is my mate," Eric growled, his eyes glowing again. Hades considered the alpha. At first, it seemed he wasn't impressed by Eric's rage, but he was; Chris had seen it in the man's eyes. Chris inwardly chuckled when he felt his father's rage surface. The walls began to shake as Eric's rage was building and building. "Father? Please, don't kill us," Carmen said in a raised voice. She had to raise her voice because the sound Eric produced was slowly becoming deafening.

Ares stood, arms crossed over his muscled chest, watching an alarmed-looking Hades. Hades and Ares hated each other, and it had started so long ago that no one knew why. However, it was evident that Ares liked an uncertain-looking Hades. It was something that had never happened before, especially in the underworld where Hades ruled.

"It seemed that this time you bit more than you can swallow, Hades," Ares grinned. "Call him off," Hades growled, and was that fear in his eyes? "Well, since he is my brother-in-law and super powerful, as you surely have noticed by now, I can't call him off. Return his mate and Shawn, and maybe, just maybe, he won't destroy the underworld." "No," Hades said, and Ares was impressed by the underworld ruler's answer.

"Return my father and Shawn, or face the consequences," Chris said as he moved until he stood next to Eric. Then his power found Eric's, and together they began tearing the underworld apart. "Stop! Alright, alright," Hades growled as the walls began to crumble under their combined powers.

Chapter Seventeen

"I can't believe it," Jory said, voice shaky. "I will kill him for this," Damian growled. "We let Hades be for now because Shawn needs us; he needs *you*," Dacian said. No one argued with the archangel because they knew Hades couldn't be killed. However, Eric and the four should be able to hurt him.

"I can't figure out what's wrong with him," Jack said as he gently closed the door to the room Shawn was lying in. "What do you mean you don't know?" Damian growled, fangs showing. Eric took Damian by the arm and guided him into Shawn's room.

They had managed to get Jory and Shawn out of the underworld by threatening to destroy the place. Eric had joined forces with his powerful son, and together they had begun to tear down the walls of Hades' living quarters. Hades had no other choice than to release Shawn and Jory.

The ruler of the underworld knew that he couldn't be killed, but when he had seen the power of Eric and Chris combined, he had no choice but to relent. However, somehow Shawn had lost consciousness and hadn't regained it again. Jack had examined Damian's beloved but couldn't find anything wrong. Jory had come back unharmed, much to Eric's relief. If it had been Jory instead of Shawn, Eric and Chris probably would have destroyed the underworld, with Hades in it.

As it was, Shawn was the one who had been harmed, and no one knew how it had happened. But Hades had claimed that it wasn't him, and somehow, Eric had believed him. So, who managed to get to Shawn while the man was in the underworld where nothing happened without Hades knowing about it? But, the ruler of the underworld had denied having anything to do with Shawn's condition.

"There must be something we can do," Grace whispered. Chris sighed because he was out of ideas, which didn't sit well. He was getting angrier by the hour because Shawn's condition seemed to worsen. The thought of Shawn not surviving the ordeal was killing Chris.

They heard Damian praying for whoever would listen to save his beloved's life; it was something that made Chris even angrier. Chris had returned to the underworld to question Hades about Shawn's condition. The ruler had claimed that no one, absolutely no one, could have breached the security without him noticing it.

Or Hades was lying because admitting that someone had managed to penetrate the wall of security and harm Shawn had been possible. Or he really was just as baffled as he pretended to be. But unfortunately, Chris hadn't been able to read Hades.

Jory had looked into Shawn's head and had found it hard to access the man's brain. The alpha mate had encountered a barrier. Jory had seen an obstacle, which he suspected was planted to prevent Shawn from waking up. Jory knew that it didn't look good, but there was nothing he could do, which made him very angry. It was seldom that he had felt so helpless.

"I have to talk to my mate; I'll be back soon," Eric said as he lightly squeezed Damian's shoulder. The master vampire didn't even look up but had all his attention on Shawn.

"We need to do something because if we don't, he won't survive," the alpha whispered as he sat down next to Jory, wrapped his arms around his mate, and held him tightly. "We will, babe. We will," Jory mumbled into Eric's broad chest.

Suddenly the air began to move, and a moment later, three women dressed in dark blue appeared. Eric and Jory immediately jumped from the couch, ready to defend. "No," Chris said, but he hadn't spoken to his dads but to the three women.

"I'm afraid so," the one to the left said, her voice gently, almost soothing. Eric looked from one to the other; he said in a not-so-friendly tone, "Can someone tell me what's going on?" "Let me introduce the three fates." Pointing to the first woman, he said, "This is

Clotho; she is the one who spins the thread of life. She is the beginning of life, as you could call it. Then we have Lachesis; she assigns each person a thread. Then last but not least, meet Atropos, and we don't want her here," Chris eyed Atropos and said, "It's nothing personal." She nodded. "Atropos snips the thread of life at its end," Chris added softly.

Jory nodded because he knew about the three sisters. Gaia had explained about the three fates when Eric had been shot and needed both Jory and Chris to heal him. Even though the alpha mate's heart was racing, he kept quiet.

"No, you can not take Shawn. I won't let you take him," Jory said as he stepped away from Eric. Clotho held up her hand. "We are not the enemy. Shawn's life has come to an end, and that we're here is of courtesy to you, alpha of the Wentworth Pack and The four. When she said The Four, she meant Chris, Carmen, Grace, and Marcus. It was what they were called in the magical community. When the clock strikes twelve, we will descend and help Shawn to cross over." Her tone was calm and soothing. Before any of them could react, the three fates had vanished.

"I can heal him." All eyes were on Carmen. "What?" Eric said. "I said I can heal him," Carmen repeated patiently. "Sweetheart, as much as I want Shawn to survive, we can't defy death," Eric warned. "I don't want Shawn to die, not only because I like him, but I also don't want to see Damian destroyed over it," Carmen insisted.

Eric sighed and knew that he couldn't stop his daughter. "Just be careful, sweetheart," the alpha warned. "Do you need us to be in the room with you?" Jory asked. Carmen shook her head. "No, I'll be alright. Gaia granted me powerful healing powers," she eyed Jory and said, grinning, "Even more powerful than yours."

Carmen softly knocked and carefully opened the door to Shawn's room. If she had any doubts about healing Shawn, then they were gone now. Damian sat on the floor, silently praying, and Carmen saw a broken man. "Damian?" Carmen gently touched the vampire's shoulder.

Damian looked up, and Carmen's heart broke when she saw the devastation in his eyes. Here was a man who knew he was about to lose his beloved, the most precious person in his life. "I can heal Shawn," she softly said. "How?" Damian's response was weak, like the man had given up. "If it's alright with you, I will heal Shawn." Carmen didn't say that she probably, well, very likely would be punished for what she was about to do. "You have my permission to try," he said in a barely audible voice.

Carmen pulled the cover away and looked at Damian. "I have to remove his shirt," she softly said. "Just do what you need to do, please," the vampire said. Carmen could tell he didn't believe she would pull it off.

Carmen carefully removed his shirt. Then, she leaned over him and began to quietly mumble words Damian couldn't decipher, not that the master vampire was listening. Damian had only eyes for his beloved, who still lay motionless on the bed.

After about thirty minutes, Carmen opened her eyes and stepped away from the bed. Damian looked up, and the moment Shawn opened his eyes, Carmen lost consciousness. Damian was just in time to catch her as he yelled for Eric and Jory. Within seconds the alpha and his mate rushed into the room. "Shit! No no no," Jory whispered as he saw Carmen lying on the bed where Shawn had been just moments ago.

Shawn stood next to Damian, who had his arm tightly wrapped around his beloved. Eric turned to the master vampire. "What happened?" he questioned. Damian shook his head. "Carmen came into the room and said that she could heal Shawn. So, I gave her permission that she could do what needed to be done to heal him. But unfortunately, the moment he opened his eyes, Carmen lost consciousness. I really don't know what caused it. At first, I thought that she had drained herself. But now it seems more severe," the master vampire replied. Even though he was over the moon that Shawn was saved, he was sad because they didn't know why Carmen didn't wake.

Damian and Shawn returned to the coven, but the master vampire had said several times that, if they ever needed the coven, for whatever reason, he would comply. Damian had said that he was forever in their debt. Eric had told him they had helped the master vampire because they were friends, which created no obligations. Nonetheless, Damian had insisted, so Eric had finally given in.

"She's in a coma," Dacian said. Eric growled; Jory's expression let them know he wouldn't accept his daughter's condition. "What are your plans to get Carmen back?" Chris asked. The man had been very quiet, too quiet, which was never a good sign.

"I don't know, but I'll figure something out," the alpha mate said as he gently stroked his daughter's hair. "Can't you reach her? After all, you share a mind link," Finn asked. "I've tried already, no luck. It's like she's not there anymore. I can't explain the feeling when I tried to enter her mind," Chris sighed.

Chris had even joined forces with Marcus and Grace in an effort to reach his sister. However, it was to no avail; somehow, someone had managed to seal Carmen's mind, so no one would be able to reach her.

Chris was beside himself because, as The four, they were connected to each other's minds and souls. So, that he couldn't reach her was driving Chris slowly insane. That was the downside of being connected to each other. Fuck with one meant fuck with the rest as well. Was that what they tried to achieve? Driving Chris insane? Marcus and Grace weren't as affected as Chris because even though they were siblings, Chris was closest to Carmen.

Gaia had explained that they were siblings, even though they had different parents. It was because they had been created, not born.

Chapter Eighteen

The air moved, and Clotho materialized. "What the fuck is wrong with my daughter?" Eric growled, his eyes glowing again, which was never a good sign. Clotho, however, didn't seem impressed by Eric's outburst. She eyed everyone in the room before she finally spoke.

"Carmen knew not to intervene with Atropos. We have warned her that a day like this would come, and she would lose a friend. We told her if Atropos would come for someone, we don't condone interference from anyone, including her. Yet, she did it anyway by saving Shawn's life, even though it was his time to leave this earth."

"So, you put her in a coma as a way of punishment?" Eric's growl was even more profound and menacing. "No, that wasn't me; we don't have the ability to put anyone into eternal sleep," she said matter of factly.

"Excuse me. Did you say eternal sleep? What does that mean?" It was the alpha mate who spoke, and Eric and Chris both knew that the tone Jory used meant nothing good. "It means that Carmen will sleep forever," Clotho explained.

"No! It's not acceptable. You wake her up, right this minute," the alpha mate's voice was very low, which meant that Jory was close to losing it. *Baby? Calm down, please? It won't do our daughter any good if you attack Clotho. We need to figure out how to wake her up without starting a war between us and the fates.*" Jory reared back at feeling the sudden warmth of Eric's presence flowing through his mind. He knew that his mate was right, but it took some effort and a lot of willpower to calm down.

Dacian entered the room and gently touched his grandson's shoulder, which calmed Jory even further. He greeted Clotho, and Jory noticed the archangel's tone was friendly. Now, why the hell was he acting friendly with the youngest of the Three Fates?

"I came here to let you know what was going on with Carmen. My job here is done," Clotho said and was about to vanish when Dacian stopped her. "Who put Carmen into eternal sleep?" the archangel questioned. Clotho looked over her shoulder. "Hypnos," she said, and then she was gone.

The question now was, who was this Hypnos, and who had ordered him to put Carmen in a coma? Well, whoever it was, he would have to answer to Chris. The first in line to succeed Eric as alpha should his father fall ill, or worse, die.

Even though they still hadn't talked about it, everyone automatically assumed that if something happened to Eric, Chris would take over the pack. After all, he was the firstborn of the alpha and alpha mate.

"So, let's find, what's his name again?" "Hypnos," Dacian said helpfully. "Yeah, him. Let's find him and force him to wake up Carmen," Jory insisted. "Why are you looking like that?" the alpha mate asked when he saw the dark expression on his grandfather's face. "I doubt that we would be able to track down Hypnos because no one has seen him for centuries," Finn mixed himself into the conversation.

"Well, no one, except the one who ordered him to put my sister in a freaking coma," Chris, who had joined his fathers, said. "Where is Sarah?" Jory asked when he saw she wasn't at the angel's side. "She's with Rose and the baby," Finn said as he smiled. Jory smiled too because his father still was very much in love with Sarah.

Armand and JJ stepped into the room as well. Eric had initially been against Armand and JJ's relationship because he knew what Armand was like. The angel had many conquests to his credit. And lots of one-night stands. Eric knew how fragile JJ was when it came to relationships. Plus, the alpha thought JJ was still too young. However, against all odds, Armand was committed to his relationship with Jordan.

The same was true for Emma and Ares, the God of War, because before meeting Emma, Ares had a reputation of being a notorious womanizer. He had even taken men to his bed. However, after meeting and falling in love with Emma, he changed into a serious and loving partner. Ares, like Armand, had shown himself worthy of being included in the pack. Armand, even though being an angel, had become a pack member because he and Jordan Jones were mated. Ares, although God of War, would become a pack member as well after he and Emma were mated.

Ares had wanted to make Emma his for some time now, but the alpha's sister had been reluctant. She wanted to go on an actual honeymoon after their mating. As things were right now, she couldn't leave the ranch because everyone was needed in the war against Zachariah, Dhidysus, and Leldur. Eric was delighted to see that Ares had the patience of a, well, saint when it concerned Emma.

Armand eyed Chris. "Now that Carmen is in a coma, doesn't that weaken the three of you?" the angel asked. Suddenly, all eyes were on Armand and JJ. "What? Have none of you thought about that possibility? What if that was precisely what they wanted to achieve? Weaken you, Chris, because we know it's still all about you. Zachariah wants you, so he can try and take your powers. As The four, you practically are unbeatable. Now, Carmen is in some sort of coma, which must weaken the three of you. It's only logical," JJ said.

"Shit, you could be right, and that means we must ready ourselves for another attack," Chris said. "Well, that's reason enough to find Hypnos so that he can wake Carmen up," Grace said. "I already told you that it will nearly be impossible to contact him," Dacian said. "Then, let's find someone who can lift whatever it was that Hypnos did to Carmen and wake her up," Grace said.

Dacian grinned evilly; he said, "And I know just the man who could help us to accomplish that." "Oh, no. Not *him*," Ares groaned. "Oh yes, *him*," the archangel chuckled. "Who?" Eric, Jory, Max, and

James asked in unison. "Zeus," Dacian and Ares said simultaneously. "Are you kidding me? You actually mean *the Zeus*," Jory whispered, then he eyed Ares. "The Zeus, as in, your father?" the alpha questioned. "The very same," Ares said, and he didn't look happy.

Emma, who, together with Ares, had joined the others, looked from Ares to Jory. "There's so much I don't know about you, my love," she said. Ares looked at Emma with so much tenderness it made Eric smile. "I'll answer all of your questions later, sweetheart," Ares said as he gently kissed her lips.

"Yeah, but would he want to help? I mean, he is your father, right?" Emma asked. "Oh yes, he will help us because he hates Hypnos," Dacian answered before Ares could.

"And why's that?" Eric questioned because the alpha didn't know Hypnos, or any of them, which meant he didn't trust them. Eric was cautious about trusting people, the Gods, or whoever if he didn't know them.

"We have no other choice than to reach out to Zeus; he's the only one who could undo Hypnos' spell and wake up Carmen," Dacian informed. "Why does Zeus hate Hypnos?" "Well, let's say Hypnos managed to trick Zeus, helping the Danaans to win the Trojan War. And then there was Hera, his wife, who hated her husband's guts. The Word is that Hypnos helped her to put Zeus to sleep. I don't know if he actually did it or was too scared because putting a mighty God like Zeus to sleep is risky. I believe it's even impossible; the man is simply too powerful. Plus, he would have destroyed Hypnos for so much as even trying to put him under a spell. So, you understand that Zeus is not too fond of Hypnos," Dacian explained, smiling.

"I don't care what his motive is; the main thing is that he helps us. So, how do we get in contact with Zeus?" Chris asked. "That's not so easy, Chris," the archangel said. Even though Zeus hates Hypnos, he will be reluctant to grant us an audience. Don't forget that he is a very mighty God and is feared by most.

"I will see what I can do to get his attention," Dacian said. "Get his attention, uh?" Chris echoed. The archangel nodded, and then he vanished. "Let's hope he manages to get Zeus' attention," Grace softly said. Chris didn't reply because if Dacian failed, he was sure he would succeed in getting the God's attention. He would enter Olympus if he had to; that would get Zeus' attention. If that weren't enough, he would start destroying everything that crossed his path.

Chris spent the rest of the day sitting at Carmen's bedside, holding her hand and praying she would open her eyes. He even softly sang lullabies that Jory used to sing for them when they were kids.

It was late in the afternoon when Jory entered the room and put a tray with hot soup and sandwiches on the small round table in the far corner. "You need to eat something," the alpha mate urged. Chris shook his head, "Thanks, dad, but I'm not hungry," he said. "You need to keep up your strength, and by not eating, you're weakening yourself, which is stupid," Jory said matter-of-factly.

"I made your favorite vegetable soup with a lot of veggies," Jory said as he took his son's arm and gently guided him to the table. Jory was about to pull the chair back when Chris stopped him. "I'm capable of pulling a chair back," he chuckled.

Chris finished his bowl of soup and ate the three sandwiches Jory had made. Since Chris was a vegetarian, the sandwiches were meatless. Chris looked up at his father. "Did you get it from Carmen's vegetable garden?" "Yes, I know that you like fresh tomatoes and other toppings on your sandwich. So, I went into the garden and took what I needed," the alpha mate said. That earned him a smile from his son, and it reached his eyes, which pleased Jory to no end. He was worried about Chris' mental state because he had never been without his sister. Jory hoped and prayed that Dacian, his grandfather, would return soon with good news.

Jory liked that his son didn't eat meat because he was a vegetarian. Eric had once said that Chris looked a lot like Jory. Chris looked up,

"Dacian has returned," he said as he stood, and together, they quietly left the room. Both men were anxious to hear what the archangel had to say.

Before they closed the door, Chris turned and eyed his sister for a few minutes. Hoping that he would see a movement, even if it was a twitching of her fingers. Nothing happened, and a dejected Chris left the room and followed Jory down the stairs and into the living room.

Chapter Nineteen

"I'm sorry," Dacian said. "Don't apologize for something that's not your fault," Eric said as he squeezed the archangel's shoulder. "So, that means if we can't get a hold of Zeus, Carmen might never wake again?" Chris seethed.

"We are the children of the Gods, at least that's what they call us. However, now that we need them, no one comes to aid Carmen?" Grace sounded furious; her eyes were practically shooting fire.

"I'll get a hold of Zeus if I have to destroy Olympus to do it," Chris said, and then before anyone could react, he was gone. "How did he do that? I mean, he's so quick," Jory whispered. "Right now, I wish I was with Chris to help him," Grace said, and then was gone too. "What the hell is going on?" Eric eyed Marcus because he was the only one still in the living room.

"Me too," Marcus said, meaning that he wished to be with his sister and Chris. And whoops, then he was gone as well. "I think I'm going to faint said Rose, who stood in the doorway, Caitlin in her arms. "Please, don't faint, honey," Alex said as he looked at Eric and Jory for help." "Oh, get a grip; Rose doesn't faint that easily," Jory grinned right before his expression turned serious again.

"We have to trust that Chris doesn't do anything stupid," Eric softly said as he wrapped Jory into his arms and held him tightly. "That's the point; he's not thinking very rationally right now. His sister was put in a coma, and no one want's to help get her back. Chris is furious, and I'm afraid that fury will turn into rage," Jory replied. He leaned with his back against Eric's chest, looked over the garden, and sighed. What a freaking mess.

They frowned when what seemed like a small earthquake hit the ranch. "What was that?" JJ asked. The pack had gathered in the main house like they always did when something was up. The angels, Dacian the archangel, Annabella, Cassandra, and Ares, everyone was present.

95

"I believe that was a very angry Chris," Jory mumbled, and that was precisely what he'd been afraid of. An angry Chris would turn quickly into an enraged Chris, which was bad. Jory and Eric still had no clue of what Chris was capable of. Hell, the man himself might not even fully know what would happen when he lost control. Jory had felt Chris' rage and feared for the worst when his son disappeared without a word. He would go after Zeus, of that the alpha mate sure.

He feared for Chris not because he was afraid his son would get hurt; he was worried that his son would destroy Olympus if Zeus refused to help.

******

"Alright, you don't want to talk to me? That's fine," Chris said as he tried to keep his cool. On their way up, he fought with two creatures he couldn't place, and he pulverized them both. By killing them, Chris had unleashed so much magic he was sure they must have felt it back at the ranch.

"Can it be that Zeus doesn't hear you calling for him?" Grace said. Chris shook his head. "That man sees and hears everything that's going on in the universe," he grimly replied.

The three stood what seemed on the clouds, which shouldn't be possible because clouds weren't solid; everybody knew that, right? Yet, here they were, standing on the clouds and looking at the earth far beneath them.

"Only one more step, and we should reach Olympus," Marcus said. "Well, then, let's do it," Grace replied. They held hands as Chris closed his eyes, concentrating on Olympus, home of the Gods. Olympus was only accessible to the Gods, but since Chris, Marcus, and Grace had the title, Children of the Gods, they should be able to access Zeus' home without a problem. Or, Chris hoped so; he wasn't sure because they weren't Gods; they just had been created by a couple of them.

The jump to Olympus went smoothly, and when Chris opened his eyes, they stood in front of what seemed to be a gate. It was like they landed in Ancient Greece. The cast iron fence was attached to large white columns with a roaring lion on top of each. There was a fog that made everything seem blurry. They stood on a kind of plateau and were surrounded by large green trees and bushes.

The fog that surrounded them was slowly creeping upward, and Grace was the first to experience breathing difficulties. Then Marcus grabbed his chest because he, too, was running out of air.

Chris looked worriedly at Grace and Marcus when he saw they were having trouble breathing. He didn't need to think twice about who had cost these problems. Chris was sure that this was the work of Zeus. After all, the God did not want to see them.

"That you don't want to see us is one thing, but attacking us is another. So don't make me angry because you, Zeus, should know what I am capable of," Chris said in a threatening tone.

When it remained still, Chris slowly began to lose his self-control. He took a deep breath and slowly exhaled again. He needed to keep control; he could not lose control, for Chris himself did not even know exactly how much power he possessed. After all, he had not been given time to test himself, he did have memories, but somehow that was different.

Gaia and Destiny had given him all the memories he needed, from kindergarten to college to the here and now. Still, many things felt to Chris like he was experiencing them for the first time.

"This is weird, isn't it?" Grace said. Even though they hadn't been to Olympus before, they knew how to open the gate and where Zeus had his, well, quarters. It was a present from Destiny, who had planted the knowledge in their minds during their aging process.

Chris raised his arms and pointed to the gate, which disappeared in the blink of an eye. "Let's go and find Uncle Zeus," Chris said mockingly. Well, Zeus was the father of Ares, who was about to mate with their Aunt Emma. So, they might as well call him uncle. Chris chuckled at the idea of calling the man uncle to his face.

They entered Olympus, and Chris immediately felt a surge of power ripping through his body. "What the hell?" he cried out as he reared back, almost falling on his butt. "Didn't you feel that?" he asked, seeing the confused looks on Grace and Marcus' faces. "Feel what? I didn't feel anything," Grace said; eyeing her brother, she asked, "Did you?" "Nope, nothing," Marcus replied.

Then, Chris was hit by a second surge of power, and this time he went down. "Oh sweet hell," Grace growled as she knelt beside Chris while Marcus kept scanning their surroundings. "I'm alright, I'm fine," Chris panted as he stood and looked around. However, he wasn't fine because it felt like his body was on fire, and it hurt like hell.

Finally, after a few minutes, Chris was able to breathe again. "What happened just now?" Marcus asked while scanning the area, just in case someone might be so stupid as to attack them. "I'm not sure, but whatever I was hit with felt off," Chris answered.

Then he lifted his head and called Zeus. As expected, the God didn't answer. He knew that Zeus was arrogant, but nevertheless, he needed him. So he lifted his head again, and this time he didn't call for the God, but he let his power clash with some invisible barriers.

Sparks flew, and lightning came their way in the form of an electrical storm. However, Chris didn't even try to avoid it but raised his hand and waved toward the now thundering storm, sending it to where it had come from.

"Is that all you got?" Chris yelled, taunting Zeus because he knew the electrical storm could only come from him. "I'm not leaving Olympus until I have spoken to you," Chris yelled. Then, when nothing happened, Chris took Marcus and Grace's hands and focussed his power on a particular spot he suspected was the entrance to Zeus' home.

It was like a bomb had gone off, the explosion was loud, and the door became visible. "That's what I thought," Chris mumbled. The house became visible, and it looked nothing like one would expect. It was a modern, white brick two-story building. The roof tiles were dark red; it even had a veranda with colorful flowers, left and right.

Chris knew the moment Zeus was heading their way. So, he wasn't surprised or shocked when the God suddenly materialized in front of them.

Zeus was taller than Chris, the God was at least six feet and seven inches, and he was massive. And, with his shoulder-length curly hair and full beard, he was an impressive figure. As it was, Chris wasn't that impressed because he had memories of the God, so his appearance was no surprise. However, it was something that Zeus had noticed, too, because, for a second, he looked confused. "I should have known," he finally said.

"Should have known what?" Marcus questioned. "None of you are impressed by my appearance." "That's right, we aren't," Grace said defiantly. "You better show some respect, little girl," Zeus growled. "I will if you do," she said. And they saw a hint of a smile on the God's face. But, it was gone just as fast as it had come.

"What is it you want from me?" a boring-looking Zeus questioned. "I want you to lift the spell that keeps Carmen, my sister, from waking up," Chris said. Zeus looked surprised; then, his expression turned into a boring one again. "You have the nerve to disturb me for something as unimportant as that?" he said, raising his voice.

Chris was vibrating with power that begged to be unleashed; he said, "Yes, that's exactly why we're here," his voice was low and had lost almost all of its humanity. Zeus eyed Chris for a long time before he spoke again. "Just leave while I let you. Don't ever come back." These weren't the words Chris had hoped to hear as his anger rose to a dangerous level, making his body vibrate even harder.

Zeus looked alarmed when Olympus began to shake. However, he didn't react, which enraged Chris even further. This time, he directed his power directly at Zeus' house and began tearing down the walls. That got the reaction he had hoped for. Zeus' eyes shot rays of fire toward Marcus, Grace, and Chris.

Chris managed to stop the fire from reaching them and instead sent it back to Zeus. "What the? How did you do that? It shouldn't be possible," he whispered, clearly impressed by Chris' powers.

"We are the Children of the Gods, and you should know that, together, we're nearly unbeatable. However, as it is, Hypnos put a spell on Carmen, putting her in eternal sleep. I need you to wake her up," Chris explained, his voice letting everyone know that he was done reasoning with Zeus.

"Wait? Did you say Hypnos?" Zeus'growl was low and dangerous when he spoke the name of the man he hated deeply. "Well, yes. Do you know him?" Chris asked, sounding innocent now. Of course, he knew about the history between the two men.

"Bring your sister here, and I'll lift the spell. And, please, don't destroy anything else," Zeus growled as he turned and shut the door in their faces. "That was odd," said Marcus. "It was, but he will help us, and that's the only thing that counts," Chris replied.

Chapter Twenty

"Are you sure that it's safe for Carmen?" Max asked her son because she was concerned about Carmen's safety. The tiger shifter loved all four equally. Maybe it was because, in a way, The four were siblings since the Gods had created them. "Yes, mother, Zeus will keep his word, of that we're sure," Marcus said. Max nodded. "Alright, I'll have to trust your instincts," she said.

"You really tore down the walls of Zeus' home?" a proud-looking Eric asked. "I didn't mean to, but I was so full of rage. That damn God is so arrogant," Chris said. "That he is," Dacian chuckled. "We clashed once or twice, but that's more than two hundred years back. However, Zeus never forgot, and he still doesn't like me," the archangel admitted.

"Do you need us to accompany you?" Felicia asked. Chris shook his head, "No, thanks. I hope to be back within a couple of hours," he replied. Jory and Eric didn't look happy because if anything happened, they probably weren't able to protect their children.

Chris headed for Carmen's room and was followed by Marcus and Grace. They didn't approach the bed when they entered the room but kept their distance. "Even now, I feel her power," Grace whispered. Chris cocked his head because something wasn't right. He called for Jory, who was at his side in seconds, Eric hot on his heels.

The moment the alpha mate stepped into the room, he felt it. Jory didn't need an explanation because he knew something was terribly wrong. His daughter was surrounded by what looked like a cloud but not quite.

"Can you see anything?" Chris asked quietly. Jory nodded and explained what it was he saw surrounding Carmen. "This wasn't here one hour ago when I checked on her," he said. *Dad? Help me, please?* Jory nearly fell on his ass as Carmen's pleading voice forcefully entered his mind. He grabbed his head and fell to his knees. "Baby? What's wrong? What happened," Eric growled as he scanned the room for intruders.

"Shit! That hurt," Jory whispered as he braced himself for another attack from his daughter. It was evident that Carmen hadn't been able to control the invasion because otherwise, it hadn't hurt so much. Carmen had screamed for help, and that had hurt like a bitch.

"That was Carmen. She aggressively entered my mind. I could tell that she wasn't able to control it. That's why it hurt so much," Jory explained. "What did she say?" the alpha asked, looking hopeful. "It was a cry for help," Jory said as he slowly pushed himself up. His knees still were a bit shaky, but other than that, he was okay.

"She's running out of time," Chris said, "We need to hurry," he added as he reached for his sister to lift her into his arms. However, the moment he touched her, Chris was thrown back, and he hit the wall hard. "What the hell?" he cursed as he moved toward the bed again.

"Stop, Chris. There's a reason you can't take her to Zeus," Ares, who had followed Emma into the room, said. "Someone is preventing you from bringing her to Olympus so he can lift the spell. So, now we have to find out who is blocking you," Ares added at seeing the confused expression on Chris' face.

Chris nodded and had a pretty good idea who was blocking him. "Hypnos," he growled. "I guess so," Ares agreed. Chris was silent for a long time, startling everyone when he finally spoke. "I want him destroyed," he softly growled, then he was gone. "Oh sweet hell," Grace said as she too vanished, followed by Marcus.

Eric called Armand to guard Carmen, just in case. JJ was tending the horses; he would join Armand later. They went downstairs and into the living room, where Max and James were quietly talking to each other.

"I hope they return soon and that Zeus really wants to lift the curse," Max said. Then she saw Jory's grim expression. "What's wrong?"

the white tiger questioned in alarm. Jory told her and James what had happened when Chris had tried to lift Carmen from the bed.

"So, where are they? Where did they go?" Max demanded. Jory shrugged. "Your guess is as good as mine," he replied as he stared out the window at the passing clouds. He prayed that the children would be safe. Jory also knew that Chris wouldn't rest until he had Hypnos.

******

"I can smell him. He was here not too long ago," Chris growled. "We smell him too. Let's go and follow the trail now that it's still fresh," Grace said. The three had followed Hypnos' scent all day, and they were getting closer.

Chris had no idea how long he was gone from the ranch, and he didn't care. All he wanted was to capture Hypnos and beat him to a pulp. Chris hoped the bastard would fight back, so he had reason to kill him. Well, come to think of that, Chris had every reason to end the bastard's miserable existence. After all, he had put Carmen in an eternal sleep, the rat. So yes, he would end his life because he had every right to do so.

"This smells funny," Grace said as she sniffed the air. Chris and Marcus eyed her with curiosity. "I don't smell anything," Chris said; looking at Marcus, he asked, "Do you?" Marcus sniffed the air, and then he shook his head because he didn't smell anything either.

"It's strange because I think we lost Hypnos' trace," Chris said. He hoped he was wrong but feared that he was right, they not only had lost Hypnos' trace, but Chris didn't know where they were. Marcus eyed Chris; he said matter of factly, "We are lost, aren't we?"

"I'm afraid we're not in Kansas anymore." It was Grace who came up with the solution. "Of course, that's it. The Wizard of Oz," she said. Both men looked at her like she was from another planet. "What are you talking about?" Marcus asked, "Oh, didn't you see the movie? It was great. I watched it at least ten times. We need to hold hands, and then we need to know where we want to go," she said, her eyes were twinkling like two bright stars.

Chris looked thoughtful because where did they want to go next? They had lost Hypnos' trace, and Chris had no clue where to search for the bastard. "I think we need to go home, to the ranch. Because we need to regroup, and then we decide how to go from there," he said. Chris didn't like it, but he felt like he had no other choice than to go home for now.

They held hands and focussed their minds on the ranch, on their parents, who would be anxiously waiting for them to return. And, of course, the pack, which would be worried as well. When they opened their eyes, they were back at the ranch, or so it seemed. "What the fuck?" Chris growled when he saw creatures he couldn't identify coming toward them. "Shit, what are they?" Grace said as she readied for battle. At first, Chris thought that the ranch was under attack. However, it quickly became apparent that they hadn't made it to the ranch. Well, not the ranch they called home. So, where were they?

Marcus and Chris were about to unleash their powers when the creatures from hell suddenly vanished. "What the?" Chris didn't get the chance to finish what he was about to say when out of nowhere, Hypnos appeared. "Let's kill him," Marcus growled, but Chris' hand on his arm stopped him. "I think that this isn't real. If my memory is correct, then we are in some sort of parallel world. Don't you have that memory?"

Marcus and Grace shook their heads because, no, they didn't have a memory of a parallel world, which was strange. They thought all four of them would get the same memories if it were about knowledge of other worlds.

"Watch this," Chris said as he waved his hand and yelled, "Be gone." And, lo and behold, Hypnos became transparent and vanished altogether. "So," Marcus said, "Do you actually know where we are?" "I certainly do. We are in a parallel world," Chris chuckled; he just couldn't help himself. It was the tension and the stress that finally got to him.

Marcus and Grace eyed each other. "It's about time. We thought that with the aging they took your humanity too," Marcus said. "He's right, you know. Most of the time, you act like a robot until now," Grace chimed in.

Chris sighed because Gaia had taken him away from the others because of what she had to say. But, what no one knew, Gaia had warned Chris to guard and protect Marcus and Grace because they weren't as strong and powerful as he and his sister. That was because their parents, Max and James, weren't as powerful as power couple Eric and Jory.

However, Grace and Marcus were powerful in their own right, and both were a force to be reckoned with. That was the reason that Chris was always on his guard and saw to it that Grace and Marcus were kept safe. However, he also knew that they needed to get away as soon as possible because this was a dangerous world and, for the most part, unknown to them.

"We need to get to the ranch, like right now. It's too dangerous here; who knows the next person we see is Carmen or our parents, and do we know if they are real or not? We can't kill anyone in this world until we know for sure that they aren't our family members. They could be our real family or creatures who were sent to kill us," Chris warned.

They held hands and closed their eyes again. This time they landed in the small meadow where Beau was happily grazing. The horse looked up and immediately ran toward Chris. "Hey boy, is everything alright? You go and eat some of the fine grass, and I'll be back later," Chris soothed.

They walked up to the house and were stunned to see a crying Max, a worried-looking James, Eric, and Jory. "What's wrong? Was there an attack while we were gone?" Chris asked in alarm. They were hugged and kissed until Chris pulled away. "Something is wrong," he said as he carefully backed away from Eric and Jory. "I need to check to know if you really are my fathers," Chris said. Eric and Jory looked confused but nodded. "Do what you need to do, son," Eric said. After a few minutes, Chris smiled.

Chapter Twenty One

"Can you repeat that, please?" Chris said because he thought he hadn't heard correctly. "Honey, the three of you were gone for nearly two weeks." Jory put his hand on his son's shoulder. "Chris, your father, went up the walls and threatened to tear the universe apart," the alpha mate said.

Chris moved toward Eric. "I'm sorry if I made you worry, but we had no idea that we were away for such a long time," he said apologetically. "He's right; to us, it seemed like an hour, maybe less," Grace said helpfully. "It seems that in the parallel world, everything is different," Marcus chimed in.

"I know, I know, son. But, we are your parents, and we worry," Eric said as he hugged

Chris tightly. Also, Chris was glad to hear that there had been no attacks during their absence. Annabella and Cassandra had secured the house with even more wards and protection spells. "I want to see Carmen," Chris softly said.

Jory and Eric followed Chris, Marcus, and Grace to Carmen's room. Chris pulled a chair to the bed and sat down. He took Carmen's hand and began softly mumbling words no one could decipher. "No Chris no," Cassandra's raised voice made everyone turn, everyone except Chris, who was focused on his sister.

The witch moved until she was beside Chris and began murmuring incomprehensible words as well. *What the hell is going on?* Jory asked his mate through their mind link. Suddenly Chris turned his head and eyed his fathers as if knowing that they had just a silent conversation with each other. Jory looked at Chris. "What were you doing to panic your nanna like that?" Jory questioned in a firm tone.

Chris, who had stopped chanting, looked up. "I was trying a spell to wake up my sister," he answered. "You were about to use dark magic, Chris. You know that we can't allow that. Even if you use it once, it will taint your soul," Cassandra said, and she didn't sound too friendly. "All I want is for my sister to wake up. Is that too much to ask?" he seethed. Jory was sure that if they hadn't been in Carmen's room, his son would have screamed his rage to the heavens.

"Listen, all of us want Carmen to wake up. However, dark magic isn't the answer, and you know that," and this time, it was Eric who spoke, his tone firm. Everyone knew what Eric was talking about when he mentioned dark magic. When Chris was a toddler, dark magic had tainted his soul. Eric and Jory had moved heaven and earth to remove the darkness in their son's soul. Ever since Chris' soul was pure, and Eric and Jory wanted it to stay that way.

Chris, who seemed to remember what his father meant, looked guilty. "I'm sorry. It won't happen again. But, you're right; I need to be careful and guard myself against the influences of dark magic." Then, he paused, looked thoughtful, and said, "I didn't expect to be so susceptible to the dark magic."

"Well, now you know, and make sure you are not tempted to use it again," Eric said as he squeezed Chris' shoulder. "Understood," Chris softly replied. He might be a very powerful creature, but he still respected the hell out of his parents and his family.

"Hey, you can touch Carmen. That could mean that we can get her away from the ranch and bring her to Zeus," Grace said, looking expectantly at Chris, who looked confused for a second. "I guess you're right," he replied.

Chris stood at Carmen's bedside; Grace and Marcus stood behind him, touching his shoulder to amplify their powers. Eric, Jory, and Dacian were watching their surroundings in case Hypnos should decide to attack. Nothing happened, and Chris vanished, Carmen tightly in his arms. "What the hell?" cursed Grace when Chris and Carmen disappeared, and she and Marcus were still in the room.

*****

Chris materialized in front of Zeus's home, and the God was already waiting for them. He glanced around and was confused when he didn't see Marcus and Grace. "They are still at the ranch. I only permitted you to enter Olympus," Zeus said as he turned and walked inside the house, followed by Chris.

"Put her on the couch, this one," Zeus motioned for the couch that stood to the right. Chris carefully lowered his sister and put a pillow under her head so she was comfortable. Zeus chuckled. "What's so funny?" Chris questioned. "You, that's what's funny. You are a Demi-God, and still, you behave like a human. Too many emotions," Zeus clarified.

Chris was so focused on his sister and for Zeus to lift the curse that he didn't realize how Zeus had called him. "I don't care what you think; just lift the spell, and I'll take her back to the ranch," he said.

Zeus shook his head; he said, "I'll allow you to leave, but not Carmen. She stays with me here at Olympus because this is her home." Chris eyed the God, and if looks could have killed, Zeus would have dropped dead right then and there. As it was, Chris' looks couldn't kill, and Zeus was a God who couldn't be killed. "Carmen is my sister, and she will return to earth with me," Chris said in a low and threatening tone while his body began to vibrate.

"Why is she so important to you? You know that because you were created, you're siblings. In the human world, you wouldn't be. So, why are you adamant about taking her home to the ranch?" Zeus asked, looking genuinely confused.

"I will tell you why I want my sister home. You can say what you want; Carmen will always be my sister. Why? Because she is, that's why," Chris snapped. He would fight Zeus if he had to because whatever happened, he wouldn't leave without his sister.

Zeus contemplated Chris for a long time and sighed when he saw the man standing protectively at his unconscious sister's side. "Don't you dare take her," Chris growled when Zeus moved toward the couch.

"I saw inside your soul and know that your love for Carmen is pure. You would fight to the death to protect her. The one who created you exceeded all my expectations. They did well," a satisfied-looking Zeus said.

"Wait? You know who it was that created me?" Chris questioned. "That's for me to know and for you to find out. I can't enlighten you," Zeus said. "Now, let's wake your sister because she slept long enough," the God added. "Well, that is if you let me near her," he chuckled. "You may approach, but if you try to harm her." "I won't; you have my word," Zeus replied. Well, Chris had to trust Zeus to keep his word, but why had he demanded that Carmen stay with him? What was it he had said? Was Olympus her home? Yeah, no, that wasn't going to happen.

Zeus leaned over Carmen and began to draw signs above her body. His lips moved, but no sound came out. Then the God stepped back, and Carmen opened her eyes. Her eyes searched and found Chris. It was evident she was relieved to see her brother with her in the room. "Where am I? What happened?" she softly asked. Carmen sounded calm; there wasn't even a hint of panic.

Chris eyed Zeus. "We will go home now. Thank you for what you did; I won't forget it," he promised. "I know because I won't let you," Zeus said, and Chris wasn't sure if the God was joking or not. Well, the spell was lifted, and his sister was awake again, and that was all that mattered for now. Chris didn't jump for joy because he first wanted away from Zeus and Olympus.

"You may leave," Zeus said. "Again, thank you. Bye," Chris said as he rose and lifted Carmen into his arms again. "Until we meet again," the God replied. Chris didn't know what to think of that, but he needed to get back to the ranch. He wondered how long he had been away from home this time.

Chris closed his eyes, and a second later, they stood in the small meadow where Beau was happily munching on a carrot. Then, the front door flew open, and Eric, Jory, James, Max, and the rest came running toward them.

"That was fast," Jory said. Carmen wiggled herself free from her brother's arms and was immediately hugged tightly by her two dads. "So, is anyone going to tell me what's going on and why I woke up in an unknown place?" she demanded.

They went inside the house; with coffee in hand, Carmen listened to Chris telling her what had happened. "That's why I long for coffee." Jory frowned. "That's what you have to say after we explained what Hypnos did to you?" he asked. Carmen raised one eyebrow as if she was surprised her father would ask such a stupid question. "Well, I hadn't had coffee for days. So, it makes sense that I long for more coffee," she replied.

"Alright, sis, how do you feel?" Chris questioned because, in all the commotion, he hadn't had the chance to ask her anything at all. "Rested," she joked. Chris sighed because that was so typical, Carmen. "Well, since you feel rested, you can help us deal with Hypnos because he needs to pay for what he did to you," Chris said. Carmen nodded because she wanted to kick that bastard's ass.

Chris eyed Jory. "Just how long was I gone?" Jory eyed Eric, who chuckled, "Maybe thirty seconds," the alpha replied. A laughing Chris shook his head because this really was bizarre. "Like you already told us, time up there is different," Jory said.

Chapter Twenty Two

"You really were at Zeus' home?" Emma asked in awe. She wanted to know everything, but Chris had little to tell because he hadn't seen much of his surroundings. Carmen couldn't relay anything at all because she didn't have time to take in her surroundings after waking up.

She still felt a bit tired and told Jory she needed more coffee. It didn't take long before The Four retreated to discuss whatever it was they needed to talk about. Eric and Jory observed their children for a long time. They didn't like being left out, but they were adults now. Anyway, there was nothing they could do about that. The important thing was that they trusted each other.

"I still don't know what to think about the children when they shut us out like they did this evening," said Jory, while he pulled his shirt over his head and took his pants off. "You are so beautiful," Eric whispered as he stepped out of the bathroom. The love and adoration in his mate's expression brought Jory nearly to his knees. "After all these years, you still find me attractive," the alpha mate whispered.

"I can't put into words how much I love you, baby," Eric said as he took Jory in his arms and kissed the living daylights out of him. The alpha let one hand slowly slide toward Jory's ass, making him shiver with need. "It's been too long," Jory whispered as he pressed their cocks together. "I need you to claim me again because I need you so much," Jory panted.

"Not as much as I need you, baby," Eric whispered. The alpha's hot breath was like a hot summer breeze sliding over Jory's sensitive skin. Suddenly, Eric lifted Jory into his arms and carried him over to the bed. Lowering him gently, Jory immediately spread his legs.

Eric stood at the end of the bed and watched his gorgeous mate, who reached for him. The alpha was naked in record time and crawled onto the bed. They lay beside each other. "It's been a while since we had time for each other," Eric said while his fingers trailed over Jory's chest, to his stomach, and finally, his cock.

However, the alpha didn't touch Jory's hard length but let his finger trail around it and then over his abdomen, back to his chest again. Eric drew small circles around Jory's right nipple before he sucked the hardening nub, making Jory squirm beneath him. The alpha mate dug his nail into Eric's back because it was all he could do not to come right then and there.

Eric bit the right nipple before he gave the left one the same treatment. Goosebumps broke out all over Jory's body. "Let me," he said as he grabbed Eric's shoulders and flipped them so the alpha was beneath him. Eric didn't mind, for they were equals both in and out of bed. Jory licked his lips when he saw Eric's heated gaze nearly burning him.

He slowly moved toward Eric's hard length while his eyes never left Eric's. "God, I want you so bad," he whispered. "Do it," the alpha growled. And Jory complied as he parted his lips and began sucking Eric's cock. He softly moaned when the taste of his mate's precum exploded. Jory let his tongue swirl around Eric's rock-hard shaft, making the alpha moan in ecstasy.

When the alpha couldn't take it anymore, he grabbed Jory's thick, black curls and pulled him up until they were eye to eye. He slammed their lips together and moaned again when he tasted himself as his tongue invaded Jory's mouth. Eric flipped them, so Jory was now lying under him. The alpha mate grinned because he knew what was to come. However, Eric positioned himself so he was lying beside Jory as he began touching him, stroking his back and Jory's inner thighs. Then Eric let his fingertips slide upward; his fingers passed Jory's leaking cock without touching it, making Jory curse.

"Touch me, Goddammit," Jory begged, and Eric gladly obliged as he wrapped his hand around Jory's hard length and gently began to stroke. "Suck me," Jory demanded. "Happy to," Eric said as he turned, parted his lips, and let his tongue swirl around the hard, leaking cock. "Oh God, yes, yes," Jory hissed as he felt heat engulf his needy shaft.

Eric somehow got hold of the lube and had even opened it without Jory noticing it. It wasn't often that they needed lubrication, but it had been a long time since they had been intimate. Because of that, Eric didn't want to risk hurting his sweet mate. Jory yelped when he felt one finger penetrate his body. He lifted his hips, a sign for Eric that he had to speed things up. "Easy, baby. I don't want to hurt you," the alpha panted while he pushed a second finger inside his precious mate.

Jory grabbed Eric's curls and pulled him in for a kiss. He needed to feel Eric in every possible way. Their tongues dueled for dominance, and it turned Eric on even more. "Please, babe, I need to feel you inside me. I'm ready, I promise," Jory whispered hoarsely. Eric needed to penetrate Jory just as much as Jory needed the alpha's cock inside him. So, Eric didn't question his mate but instead pulled his fingers back, grabbed his cock, and began slowly pushing inside Jory's welcoming body.

Jory started moving his hips until they were in sync and wrapped his legs around Eric's waist, making the alpha push in even deeper. "I love you so much; it's been such a long time," Jory groaned. "Don't remind me, my sweet mate," Eric panted as he began to push in with more force. He knew that Jory liked it rough sometimes, and he instinctively felt that now was such a time.

"Harder, babe. Please, harder. God yes, feels so good," Jory rambled, and Eric loved it when his mate was about to lose control. He had his hands left and right from Jory's head, and sweat dripped on his mate's body.

When Eric began losing his rhythm, Jory knew that his mate was close, which was good because so was he. "Come for me, babe," Jory growled as he felt the pressure building in his lower body. Eric grabbed Jory's head, and the alpha mate knew what his mate wanted. Their gazes were intense when they kept eye contact. "This is so fucking hot," Jory cried out when he felt his release splashing over his abdomen. Eric came almost simultaneously with his precious mate. He stiffened, and then he filled Jory with his hot semen, their gazes never wavering, never looking away from each other.

They lay side by side for a long time, gasping for air, tired but happy and content. "How long has it been since we were intimate?" Eric quietly asked. Jory looked thoughtful; he finally said, "I believe it was the night before Gaia came for us to place the memories in our minds." "Sweet hell. Was it that long? How can that be?" Eric was stunned because how was it possible that they didn't have sex for so many weeks? True, they hadn't been away that long from the ranch, but the worries about their children had prevented them from being intimate.

Now it was companionable silence between the alpha and his mate. Both were lost in their own thoughts. "I wish that this whole mess was over," Jory whispered. The alpha mate was afraid that their differences in how to approach this war would cause unnecessary tension between them. Carmen and Christopher were adamant that a full-frontal attack would be the best way to defeat their enemy. Of course, Grace and Marcus had agreed. However, Jory, Eric, James, and Max, had disagreed. They had left the pack members out of it because Eric didn't want to risk dividing them. Because everyone would have their own way of approaching the war.

Then Gaia's words came to mind again. "Trust each other. Only then will you survive." Then, as if he had read Eric's mind, Jory said, "We need to trust the children. The Four, as everyone now called them, seem to know what they need to do. Also, we need to trust that Gaia prepared them well for what's to come."

"You're probably right, but God damn, I can't help but feel the need to guide and protect them as if they just still were small children. I can't explain it, but I hate not being able to help and protect them. I'm a God-damned alpha, a true alpha, which should mean something,"

Eric growled, and Jory felt his mate's rage boiling. He knew that if Eric went on beating himself up like he was doing now, the rage would soon boil over, and God only knew what would happen.

Jory took Eric's face in both hands and forced him to look at him. When he had his mate's attention, Jory gently kissed him, softly saying, "You need to calm down. You can't afford to lose control because that would put our kids even more on the defensive. And that's not what we want. We want everyone to keep their cool and stay calm so we can think rationally about how to proceed."

Eric sighed as he took Jory in his arms and pulled him on top of him. "You're right, as always, baby. But, hell, it's so hard because sometimes I still see them as my little ones," the alpha explained. Jory gently smiled down at the alpha. "I think that every parent has that feeling once in a while. I know humans do. It's why our children can always come to us when they are in trouble. Because we are their parents, they will always need us for guidance and comfort in a time of need. So, in a way, they will always be our babies, our toddlers," Jory replied as he gently kissed his mate on his full, soft lips.

Eric looked mischievous when he said, "Ready for round two?" Jory nodded, "Always," he answered.

Chapter Twenty Three

"What the hell?" Jory blinked as he woke with a start. "Shit, that's Beau," Eric growled. Jory was fully awake now because the way Beau was screaming told him that something was very wrong. On their way down, they saw that Chris and Carmen were already behind them. All four were running now because the horse was screaming in terror.

Eric was fast, but Chris was quicker. He sprinted past his father and yanked the barn door open. He came to a halt so suddenly that Eric, Jory, and Carmen ran into him. "God dam, leave my horse alone, you filthy creature," Chris growled and attacked the creature before he even finished his sentence.

In the barn, right in front of Beau, stood a creature they had never seen before. Chris shifted mid-jump and changed into a huge, magnificent wolf, making his dads very proud. It was the first time Eric and Jory had seen this one. When he still was a toddler, Chris' previous wolf was beautiful and powerful; this one almost seemed unreal. He was over seven feet tall, and his head and canines were massive. Drool slid from between his teeth to the ground as he jumped the creature that looked like a mix between a hellhound and, well, a giant spider or something.

Jory stood frozen when he saw Chris shift and attack without so much as a second thought. "God dammit, the bite of that fucking beast can be poison," Jory cursed. He was about to go after his son, but Eric's hand on his arm stopped him. "Don't. Let Chris handle it; we need to trust, remember?" the alpha whispered. Jory nodded, and even though he didn't like it, he knew that Eric was right. Jory would, however, help if Chris was in trouble.

The way it looked now, it seemed that Chris didn't need help from anyone because he had the creature on the floor in seconds. He ripped his throat out and threw him aside like trash. Then, he changed back and immediately checked Beau for injuries. Thank God the horse was fine, and the animal put his head against Chris' chest.

By the time the creature was killed, and Beau checked, the pack had gathered at the barn. "We need to get rid of that, well, thing," Cassandra said, then waved with her hand, and the bloody mess and the beast were gone. "What was that creature?" JJ softly asked, but no one had an answer.

When the pack had checked the premises, everyone went inside. "I don't know what that creature was, but I smelled Zachariah all over it," Chris growled. He wanted to say more, but his phone began to ring. He smiled as he excused himself to take the call. "Must be his girlfriend," Jory whispered. "We need to invite her over for dinner soon," Jory added because he was dying to meet the woman who had captured his son's heart. "We will, baby," Eric promised.

Carmen smirked when her brother entered the room again. "I'm dining out tonight; you don't have to wait up for me," Chris joked. "Call us if you need us," Eric said. "Have fun, and next time bring her over for dinner, okay?" Jory urged. "I will," Chris promised, turned, and went to his room to shower and change.

"What do we know about her?" Jory said, frowning. It was a legitimate question because they didn't even know if she was human or not. Chris hadn't told them anything about her.

Eric looked at Jory. "Care for a quiet night at home?" the alpha winked playfully. Jory laughed; he loved to see Eric happy. There had been so much tension because Zachariah still was after Chris and had started a war over it. A war that Zachariah had started, but the pack would end it. Chris had made that vow, and he would see it through.

Even though Chris was very powerful, Eric and Jory feared he might get hurt because Zachariah had creatures from hell at his back and call. "You're thinking too hard, baby," Eric softly said as he wrapped one arm around Jory's shoulder and guided him into the garden. The alpha knew that Jory was worried that they would lose Chris. However, he wasn't about to let that happen, and neither was Jory. Together they were a powerful couple in their own right, and they would defend their family with all they had.

It was evening, and Eric and Jory had retired in front of the TV to watch a documentary about the North Pole. "What is it, baby?" Eric softly asked. Jory was restless, and the alpha felt it, too, because of the bond they had as mates.

"I don't know; it's probably nothing," Jory said. "Tell me," Eric urged. "It's just; I don't like it when Chris is away on his own. He meets with his girlfriend, who is foreign to us. We know her name, but that's all. Why is he so secretive?" Jory said as he nestled into Eric's chest.

"We will urge Chris to bring her to the ranch for dinner, so we can finally meet her. And I understand Chris; he probably wants to get to know her before letting us meet her. It's better than if he brings all his conquests home for us to meet," Eric chuckled. Jory shot upright because that thought hadn't come to mind. "Oh, hell, that wouldn't be good," he agreed. Then, he leaned into Eric again, and they watched the rest of the documentary in silence.

Jory opened his eyes when he heard a door quietly close. Chris was careful, but Jory always knew when he got home. However, this time was different, and he swung his legs over the edge of the bed and moved to the door. "Where are you going?" Eric's voice made him stop. Jory sighed; he should have known that Eric would wake up if he left the bed. The alpha was always on his guard.

"I'm checking on Chris because I heard his bedroom door close," Jory explained. "Really? Why don't you let him be? Chris is probably tired and wants to sleep," Eric said. "Just a peek inside and check if he's alright." The worry in Jory's voice alarmed Eric, and he got out of bed as well.

"What has you so worried?" "I don't know; it's just a feeling," Jory replied as both walked into the hall toward Chris' room. Instead of Chris, they found Carmen inside Chris' bedroom. "Why aren't you sleeping?" Eric questioned when he saw Carmen sitting on the edge of the bed. She looked up at her dads. "I guess for the same reason you are," she softly replied.

"Is something wrong? Is your brother in danger?" Jory questioned. "No, on the contrary. He's well," Carmen paused; she blushed when she added, "He's very happy at the moment." Jory frowned, and then it clicked. "Oh no, don't tell me you sense it when he is with her," the alpha mate whispered. Carmen nodded. "Unfortunately, yes. It disappears when I'm in his bedroom. It's so strange," she explained.

"Did you just come into the room?" Jory asked. Carmen shook her head. "No, I just went to my room to get my lemonade," she said, holding the glass in front of Jory. "I heard the door close and thought Chris had come home," Jory explained. "I wouldn't count on him coming home soon. He will be here in the morning, though," Carmen said. "It means that he probably spends the night with his girlfriend," Eric said after seeing the confused look on Jory's face.

The alpha mate looked not happy. "Ugh, I wish you were still small children. I don't like the adult Chris," he admitted. Carmen smiled; she knew how protective her dads were, especially Jory. "He will be fine," she soothed. Jory gave her a look that said, really? "Well, goodnight, sweetheart," Jory said as he kissed Carmen's forehead.

At breakfast the following day, it was only Eric and Jory. Carmen had gotten up early to go for a horseback ride. Devon and his wife were away for a few days. The rest of the pack had their chores because there was still work that had to be done, even though they didn't breed horses anymore. Eric had decided it was too risky and feared the animals would get hurt in the war with Zachariah. Only their own horses had stayed; the rest were sold.

"Good morning," Emma greeted as she strode into the kitchen and straight to the coffee machine. "There goes our quiet breakfast," Eric joked. Jory kept looking at the entrance, expecting Ares to come after Emma. The two had been inseparable since their mating. "Where is Ares?" Jory asked because it was odd that the God of War wasn't guarding his mate.

"Oh, he is on his way," said Emma and moaned when she took the first sip of her coffee. "There's nothing better than that first taste of hot, strong coffee," she said, smiling. Ares entered the kitchen and greeted Eric and Jory as he also went to the coffee machine.

"*Beware, the attack will take place soon. Get Chris because you will need him. Trust him. Trust The Four. Don't stand in his way. Listen to him. Heed my warning, and stay alive. Ignore me, and die.*" Jory, who hadn't expected a voice, stood, reared back, and fell on his ass. Eric was beside his mate in a second. "What happened? Are you alright?" he questioned while helping Jory to his feet.

"Oh no," Jory moaned when he felt another invasion coming, and he wasn't mistaken. The voice spoke again; this time, they were words Jory didn't want to hear. "*Get your son. Chris is in danger.*" "Shit! Where is Chris? And Carmen needs to return as quickly as possible," Jory said. "I'll call her," Eric said as he grabbed his phone. "Where the hell is Christopher," Jory growled. He told Eric about the second message he heard inside his head.

"Close your eyes and concentrate on our son. You can do it, baby," Eric encouraged. And because Jory was too anxious to concentrate on anything because he was worried sick. "If anything happens to him, I'll tear the world apart," Jory roared; he was full of rage after hearing that last message. So his son was in danger, God damn!

Chapter Twenty Four

"Hey, gorgeous," Chris said as he took Alyssa in his arms and kissed her passionately on the lips. "Hey you," Alyssa panted as Chris finally broke the kiss. He smiled as he stroked a strain of raven black hair out of her face and stared into her beautiful dark green eyes.

"What smells so good?" Chris asked while sniffing the air. Alyssa smiled; she softly said, "I made vegetable soup," she eyed the oven, "Could you take the bread rolls out, please?" Chris nodded as he took the oven mitts.

He put the rack on the counter so the bread rolls could cool. The delicious smell of the soup made Chris' stomach growl; it wanted food. She eyed him. "Is there ever a time that you're not hungry?" she laughed. "I believe not," Chris replied as he took her in his arms again and kissed her gently on the top of her head.

"So, my dads are eager to meet you," Chris said between two spoons of soup. Alyssa paled. "I. I don't know if I'm ready to meet them," she replied, and Chris noticed that she sounded unsure. They finished eating in silence; Chris didn't understand why Alyssa didn't want to meet his family. Well, maybe she wasn't ready for the next step.

It was different with Chris because he thought Alyssa was the one. So, he felt he didn't need time; he wanted to mate and settle down. However, Alyssa was human, and that was probably the reason that she wasn't ready to meet his family. Jory had explained that humans were very different from shifters. So, even though he didn't like it, Chris knew he had to be patient with his girlfriend.

"Are you mad at me?" Alyssa asked carefully. Chris frowned. "No, sweetheart. Why would I be mad at you," he questioned because he had no idea. "Well, because I don't feel ready to meet your folks," she replied.

Chris took her into his arms and pressed her close to his body. "No," he whispered, "I'm not mad. You need more time, and that's okay. No pressure," he assured her. Alyssa sighed and nestled even closer into Chris' chest. They sat in silence for a long time, just enjoying the closeness.

"What's it like to grow up on a ranch?" Alyssa suddenly asked. Chris sighed in contentment while thinking of how to answer her. "I like living at the ranch, the fresh smell of the woods and the horses, even the chickens. It's better than breathing in the city's pollution," Chris answered.

"So, you don't like the city?" "No, I don't. It's too crowded, and the air smells bad. Plus, I would miss nature," Chris replied. "Would you be willing to move to the city?" Alyssa sounded careful now. Chris didn't need to think about that because, as a shifter, he knew that he would never want to live in a big city. "No." His answer was short and final.

It wasn't what he wanted to talk to her about, though. Chris longed to tell her about his family and their lives as shifters. However, Alyssa was human and didn't know about the paranormal world. So, explaining the magical world to her was something that had to wait. But, he would take what he could get, for now, anyway. Had his father faced the same problems when he had met his mate? After all, Jory had been human initially and hadn't known about shifters and alike.

For a second, Alyssa looked hostile, but she covered it quickly, and her expression changed into an unreadable one, which surprised Chris. She had looked at him with murder in her eyes; Chris was sure that he hadn't imagined that.

Alyssa climbed on his lap, grabbed Chris' hair, pulled his head back, and kissed him passionately. "Let go upstairs," she panted as she grabbed his groin. His doubts were forgotten as Chris lifted her into his arms and took the steps two at a time.

When Chris woke, he noticed that he was alone. He showered, dressed, and then descended the stairs. He expected to find Alyssa in the kitchen, drinking coffee, but the kitchen was empty. Chris searched the house but couldn't find Alyssa, which was strange because she would never leave without letting him know. Chris didn't see a note, so he had no clue where she was or when she'd left the house.

He took his phone, hit speed dial, and cursed when he got the voicemail. Shit, where was she? There was no sign of a struggle, so Chris was almost sure she wasn't kidnapped, which didn't mean he wasn't worried.

Thirty minutes later, Alyssa returned, and Chris saw the uncertainty when she saw him in the kitchen. "Hi, sweetie, you're up early," she said, smiling too brightly. "Yeah, well, I woke up, and you weren't beside me. So where did you go?" he questioned.

Alyssa's eyes darted from left to right; she avoided looking at Chris. "I was in town doing some grocery shopping," she said. Chris didn't see grocery bags, but maybe she's left them in the car. "Where are the groceries so I can bring them inside," he offered. Chris desperately wanted to believe her, but if she didn't have the bags in the car, then. No, he didn't want to go there.

"The bags are in the car; I hoped you would take them inside because they're quite heavy," Alyssa said. Part of Chris was relieved that she had spoken the truth. However, another part of him knew there was more, that she hadn't told the whole truth.

Chris went outside and opened the car to get the bags when he felt a prickling in his neck. Was he being watched? He tried to sense his surroundings without letting anyone know he was on to them. To his disappointment, he couldn't sense anyone close by. Even though it felt like he was watched, Chris didn't sense imminent danger. Maybe he was getting paranoid; who knew? With all that was going on in his life, it wasn't so strange that he was overly cautious. Chris took the bags and carried them inside, where Alyssa started putting everything away.

After she was done, she turned and smiled, and this time the smile was genuine. "What do you want for breakfast?" she asked. "Toast, scrambled eggs, and some hash browns, please," Chris said while he opened the cabinets to get plates to set the table. Next, they talked about how they would spend the day. Chris told Alyssa that he would spend the day at the ranch. Alyssa told Chris she would be in town because she had several meetings.

She asked Chris if they would have supper at her house and if he would stay the night. Chris, of course, said that he would love to spend the night at her place. Together they cleared the table, Chris put the dishes in the dishwasher, and Alyssa put away the food that was left. It all seemed so domestic, so homey. It was what Chris longed for, a place to call his own. It wasn't that he didn't like living at his parent's house because they were the best dads he could ever wish for. No, Chris wanted a family of his own, and the sudden thought came as a shock. Was that what he longed for? A family of his own, a wife and children?

Alyssa put her hands on his shoulders. "Are you alright, sweetheart?" she asked. Chris sighed and told her he was fine because what else could he say? He was ready to start a family, but he knew Alyssa was far from ready to have children. Was that also a human thing? Chris felt confused because the thought of wanting a wife and having children had stunned him. Also, Alyssa's previous behavior had thrown him off kilter. Something wasn't right, but Chris couldn't put his finger on it.

Even though Chris sensed that something was wrong, he ignored the warning.

Chapter Twenty Five

"What's wrong? Why are you looking at me like that?" Chris questioned as he got out of his car. "Where were you?" Jory growled, making Chris take a step back. He was shocked because he had never seen his dad, his sweet and kind dad, so full of rage. Chris blinked a few times; looking at Eric, he said, "I don't understand." The alpha took his son's arm and guided him away from an angry-looking Jory.

"Your dad woke in the middle of the night because he thought he heard you come home. However, when he came into your room, it was Carmen sitting on your bed. She told us that you wouldn't be home until morning. Your dad hadn't expected that, but he accepted that you would spend the night with your girlfriend, whom we really want to meet. Then, this morning, someone managed to invade your dad's mind, telling him that an attack was imminent and that we needed to get you home fast. If the attack happens, then we're supposed to let you and your siblings handle it," Eric paused, giving Chris time to comprehend.

"There's more, isn't there?" Chris softly asked. Eric nodded. "Then, shortly after the first message, the second one came along. The voice told your dad that you were in danger and that we needed to get a hold of you as soon as possible. Did something happen to make you think that, maybe, just maybe, you could be in danger?" Eric carefully questioned. They had tried to call him, but Chris hadn't answered; instead, Jory got his voicemail every time he called.

Chris shook his head. "I don't think so. Alyssa and I had dinner; then we went to her place. Nothing strange or out of the ordinary happened. I didn't sense any kind of danger, either," Chris explained how his evening went. He didn't say anything about the fantastic sex they had, but knowing his dads, he knew he didn't need to explain that to them.

"I'm sorry if I made you worry so much, dad," Chris apologized as he and Jory walked through the garden. "No, it's me who needs to apologize. I lashed out at you, and I shouldn't have done that," the alpha mate said. "Alright, now that we both apologized, I promise I will spend the nights at the ranch. For now anyway, because we're still in danger," Chris said. Jory smiled, which made Chris very happy. "I like to see you smile; you don't smile enough," Chris said.

Carmen had returned to the ranch after Eric had called her, and Chris was home as well, as were Marcus and Grace, and Jory felt like he finally could relax a bit. Emma and Sarah had made lunch for everybody, and now they were sitting in the garden, under the apple tree. The table was filled with salads, and sandwiches, with and without meat and fruit. Jory looked around and smiled; it had been too long since they all had gathered for lunch, or dinner for that matter.

"It almost feels like a normal day," Eric said, then he looked at the sky. "I miss him," the alpha softly said. "I miss Ross too," Jory whispered as he wrapped his arms around Eric's waist. Together they stood for a long time, enjoying watching their ever-growing family eat, drink, have animated conversations and have fun, people were telling jokes, and there was laughter. "It feels good to hear laughter again," said Jory. Eric nodded but didn't reply. Both men knew that, soon, the laughter would be replaced by violence and fighting for survival. "So, let them enjoy today because who knows what tomorrow brings," a somber-sounding Eric finally said. The alpha stood and motioned for Jory to follow him deeper into the garden.

"Is everything alright? You look worried," Carmen inquired. She and Chris had seen Eric and Jory going deeper into the garden. Both knew that their dads did that only when they were troubled. Carmen took Eric's right and Jory's left hand and eyed them intently. "We will get through this. Whatever comes our way, as long as we trust each other, we can conquer anything," she said. Then she kissed both her dads on their cheeks, took Chris' arm, and walked away.

Chris and Carmen joined the others, and a few minutes later, Eric and Jory joined them as well. Jory and Chris took a sandwich with vegetables on it since they were vegetarians. Jory wondered where they would stand a year from now. Would they lose pack members while at war with Zachariah, Dhidysus, and Leldur? Eric shivered at the thought of losing yet another family member.

It was why he decided to leave the pack out of the war that was coming. He wouldn't let anyone else die; he would not. Then Jory's words came to mind; they needed to trust their children. Let them fight their battles and fight Zachariah. The alpha and Jory had experienced the hard way how powerful Zachariah was. He needed to talk to Chris because he had to know if his son could pull it off to kill Zachariah if necessary.

Eric motioned for Chris to follow him, and the man did without hesitation. "What is it?" he asked as they were far enough so no one could hear them. "Soon, your great uncle will be starting the attack. I need to know if you can kill him if you get the chance," Eric asked because, as always, he was straight to the point. "Yes, there's no doubt in my mind. I won't hesitate to kill him if I can. We all know that Zachariah is practically invincible," Chris sounded firm and self-assured. "But, he can be killed," Eric said. "Yes, he can be killed. I certainly will try," Chris said. "That's good enough," Eric replied, then they returned to the others.

"Later," Eric said after seeing Jory's questioning look. He didn't want to spoil their lunch because this could be the last time with everyone at one table. Eric hoped and prayed that he wouldn't lose another family member because he wasn't sure if he could take another loss. Suddenly James stood and cleared his throat to get everyone's attention.

"Max and I have an announcement to make. We know this isn't the best time to share our news." He paused and eyed Max, who rose from her chair. "Or," she said, "This is the best time to share our news."

When everyone looked at her expectantly, she said, smiling, "We are having another baby. I'm pregnant." It stayed quiet for a second, then the table erupted, and James and Max were congratulated and hugged and kissed. Eric and Jory were the last to congratulate them. They had patiently waited until the family members had their turn.

"I'm so happy for you, Max," Jory whispered. "You look radiant; we should have noticed," Eric chuckled. "You're right; this is the best news we had in a long time. Soon we will welcome a new life into this world," Jory said. His eyes grew big as he asked, "Do you know if it's a girl or a boy?" Max smiled. "It's a girl," she grinned. "Oh, how wonderful," Jory gushed as he hugged Max again.

Chris looked up, as did Carmen, Grace, and Marcus. "Dad? Gaia is summoning us; we need to go," Chris said, and before Eric, Jory, Max, or James could react, The Four had disappeared.

They materialized in Gaia's garden, where she was already waiting for them. She didn't smile, and seeing her worried expression, Chris knew that trouble was coming their way, fast. "Within days, Zachariah will attack the ranch. The fool still wants you for your power. But, as you surely will know, Dhidysus and Leldur will also be at his side," Gaia explained.

She looked at Chris, permitting him to speak freely. "We know that Zachariah is very powerful, and combined with those two idiots, he practically is invincible. After all, they formed a triumvirate, which amplifies his power," Chris said. Gaia nodded. "Unfortunately, we can't break that bond," she said. Chris shook his head because he had expected this. "Do you have any idea how to defeat him when he is so powerful?" Chris said.

"You're right; as part of a triumvirate, Zachariah will nearly be unbeatable. However, Chaos, Destiny, and I have formed a triumvirate as well, as you know," Gaia replied. Chris nodded. "So, if we combine our powers, we should be able to stop Zachariah from using the triumvirate. That would put you both on equal ground," Mother Earth informed.

Chris smiled because this was music to his ears. "I like it," he grinned, and the other three grinned as well. "Also, I know your father has decided not to involve the pack in the coming war. But you will need Cassandra, Annabella, and even Dacian because Zachariah is his brother. The archangel could help in finding weak spots; who knows? We can take the pack away from the ranch right before the attack starts," Gaia offered.

"Rose has a small child; Caitlin still is a baby. And Max is pregnant; she needs to be protected too. I'm sure James will want to fight because that's who he is. So maybe my father should give the rest of the men and women the chance to fight Zachariah or be taken away until it's safe to return again," Chris suggested. "Wise words." The Four turned to see who had spoken.

Gaia seemed surprised. "Chaos, to what do I owe this pleasure?" she said, smiling. "Destiny will arrive soon," Chaos said. Then, looking at Chris, he said, "Zachariah is getting ready to attack the ranch; we haven't much time. Go back and let both of your dads know what you and Gaia talked about." In the blink of an eye, The Four had returned to the ranch.

"Did he say when?" Eric asked. Chris shook his head because it all happened so fast. "No, he only said that we didn't have much time because Zachariah was preparing for battle," he replied. "Then we need to do the same. I want Rose and Alex away from the ranch," Jory began. He wanted Rose safe because of Caitlin. If Rose would stay and fight, it meant that Caitlin would stay too, which wasn't an option. Jory wanted Alex, the veterinarian and Rose's mate, gone because he was human.

Then there was Jake; he was too young to fight. The rest of the pack, as well as Finn, Armand, Felicia, Annabella, Cassandra, and Dacian, would stay and help the pack defend the ranch. The alpha had talked to the pack and given them the chance to decide if they wanted to stay or leave. Jory had told Ares to take Emma and keep her safe because Ares shouldn't get involved in the upcoming battle. If he would stay and fight, it would have consequences for the God of War.

Chapter Twenty six

Chris was in full battle mode as he entered the living room. He had called his girlfriend to let her know that he had a family emergency and couldn't make it. Alyssa would have cooked for the two of them that evening, and Chris had really been looking forward to this. "There will be other evenings," Jory soothed. "I know," Chris replied absentmindedly. He wanted the whole thing over and done with, so everyone could lead a normal life again.

Chris had told his dads that he thought Alyssa was *the one*. That she was his mate. He liked both men and women and had his share of affairs, but in the end, he had fallen hard for Alyssa Knight, a human. The memories of the men and women Chris had dated were put in his mind by Destiny and Fate. To Chris, it felt real, like he actually had these affairs, and maybe he had; who knew? It should feel real because if they hadn't aged so fast, they would have experienced precisely the same memories as they now have.

"If this is over, then we want to meet Alyssa," Jory said. Chris smiled. "She's looking forward to meeting you too. She finds it cool that I have two dads, and we live at the ranch," Chris chuckled. "Is she human?" "Yes, she is. Is that a problem?" "No, of course not; we are just curious, that's all," Eric chuckled.

"Zachariah is on his way and can be here any moment," said Dacian. The archangel was still connected with his warlock brother, even though he was the good one. Chris nodded, let him come because he was ready, as were Carmen, Marcus and Grace, and the rest of their family. Cassandra had cast protection spells over everyone who still was at the ranch. And Annabella had secured the house with her most powerful spells. But Chris doubted if they would do any good because Zachariah was fucking powerful.

"I'm glad that they can't use their triumvirate against you," Jory said as he moved to the windows and peered outside. Chris didn't get time to answer. "He's here and has those two idiots and several hellhounds at his side.

Chris was outside in mere seconds. Zachariah acted immediately the moment Chris stepped outside. The warlock threw a giant demonic fireball at him, but Chris deflected the thing with ease. He sent the demonic fire back but not to Zachariah because he wouldn't be affected by it. No, he aimed straight for the hellhound that stood nearest to him.

Zachariah showed no emotions that one of his hellhounds had been vaporized by his own fireball. "And now, we will destroy you and the whole God damned pack," Zachariah yelled as he raised his hands, and both Dhidysus, who stood to his right, and Leldur, to his left, took his hand. Zachariah closed his eyes, and Chris braced himself for the impact that, lo and behold, never came. Gaia had come through for them; they managed to block the wires connecting the three as a triumvirate.

"What happened? Where is the power?" Dhidysus asked in confusion. "I don't know, you moron," Zachariah roared as he slammed Dhidysus against an invisible wall. "Your triumvirate isn't working because we blocked it," Chris laughed. He didn't tell that it actually had been Chaos, Destiny, and Gaia who had managed that. Let Zachariah think that Chris was just that powerful. "No, that's impossible because you can't have that much power. How did you do it?" Zachariah questioned, and Chris could see not only the rage in the warlock's expression but there was uncertainty as well. Chris smiled inwardly at the confusion he saw on Zachariah's face. "That's for me to know and for you to find out," he grinned.

"DIE," Zachariah yelled in rage as he threw another, and this time it was a more powerful fireball. Chris managed to deflect the demonic fireball, but this time it had left him with burn marks on his arms and chest. However, before he could assess the wounds, they had healed, and his skin was flawless again. "Nice," grinned Marcus.

"Now I'm gonna show *you* something," Chris growled as he threw a magical net over Zachariah. The warlock was so stunned that it took him some time to free himself, which gave Chris time to attack. He jumped and kicked the warlock in the chest, making him tumble backward. Zachariah managed not to fall on his ass but barely. Then he freed himself from the net Chris had thrown over him. Zachariah stretched his hand to conjure a fireball, but Chris was already on top of him, fighting him to the ground again.

Zachariah fought Chris off and pushed him back so that he could get to his feet. What the warlock hadn't expected was that Chris drew his fist back and punched him in the face, old school. It wasn't how a creature like Chris would fight. It happened so fast and was so unexpected that Zachariah, who apparently had expected magical fire or a spell thrown at him, was caught off guard and went down.

"Look at our boy; he's damn good," Jory whispered; the alpha mate was scared and proud at the same time. Afraid because he feared for his son's life, and proud because Chris was a true warrior.

However, he was immediately back on his feet again and charged. Chris began to vibrate, his shirt and jeans disappeared, and electric sparks erupted from his body. Zachariah cringed as he was thrown back; the sparks were aimed at the warlock, who wasn't able to come near Chris.

"What the hell is happening to Chris?" Eric growled as sparks flew from his son's body. "Is he getting bigger?" Jory gasped. "Yes, Chris is growing, and he gained in power," said Dacian, who was standing behind them. Jory and Eric turned, as did James and Max. All eyes were on the archangel.

"Explain," Eric demanded. Dacian frowned but didn't react to the command. He understood that everyone was on edge because of the battle that was going on. Dacian smiled as he glanced outside.

"Chris has shown that he's worthy, so Zeus gave him a bit more power to be sure that he will be able to kill Zachariah," Dacian explained.

"I don't understand because Chris is already extremely powerful, and then grant him more power?" Jory was flabbergasted and didn't know if he should be glad or concerned. Because if this was true, and Jory didn't doubt it was, then his power would be beyond imagination. He would be able to destroy half of the earth, maybe even the whole planet. However, he also was aware that absolute power could corrupt even someone as pure as Chris. His son's soul had once been tainted, and Jory didn't want to see that happen again.

Eric, Jory, James, and Max also tried to leave the house to help their children, but somehow they weren't able to get outside. Jory suspected that it was Gaia who prevented them from intervening. He hoped and prayed that their children would survive the battle.

Zachariah looked at Chris in wonder. "What are you?" he growled. Chris eyed his opponent. "I am Christopher Wentworth, shifter, son of Alpha Eric Wentworth, and Jory Bradshaw Wentworth, alpha mate. That's who I am," he growled in reply.

Zachariah began to levitate and was stunned to see that Chris was able to do the same. The air moved, sparks flew, and the earth began to shake as the two began to fight while hovering in the air. "What are you?" Zachariah asked again as he lashed out with yet another fireball; his voice had lost all of his humanity.

Chris' eyes shot fire and hit Zachariah straight in the chest, making the warlock scream in agony. "I'm the one who will end your existence; that's who I am," Chris growled. Zachariah was so thrown off guard by Chris' bold statement that his defenses went entirely down. Even if it was only for a second or two, it was what Chris had been waiting for; he reacted with the speed of light.

Chris aimed and unleashed his deadly blueish fire, and he kept targeting Zachariah, who now screamed in rage and agony. Trees fell, and the beautiful green forest turned brown, it looked like it was dying, and the wind had turned into a storm. "Oh dear God, what's happening?" Jory whispered when he saw not only the forest but their garden turn brown as well. "Holy hell, what is going on?" JJ said as he snuggled close to Armand. "We don't know," Eric answered as he kept watching his son, taking on Zachariah.

You see a very mighty, furious creature. It's like a clash of the Titans; there's too much magic in the air." Dacian whispered. Jory turned to his grandfather. "Don't tell me that my son is doing this," he said, not looking happy at all. "That's exactly what I'm saying. Chris has way more power than Zachariah, and it seems that he's toying with my brother," Dacian said as he kept watching the fight. He, too, was now unable to leave the house.

"You can't be more powerful than me; it's not possible. Chaos himself had to grant you more power, and he wouldn't do that in a million years," an enraged Zachariah seethed as he charged again. "It wasn't Chaos but Zeus who gave me some extra power," Chris said. How he knew was anyone's guess, but Chris just knew that it had been Zeus who had come to his aid.

Suddenly Chris felt a rush of power surge through his body, and he knew what it was. Zachariah, who apparently had noticed that something was going on, cocked his head. Chris' grin was an evil one. "The triumvirate," he whispered.

"No no no, not Zeus *and* the triumvirate," Zachariah screamed his rage to the heavens. "Oh yes," Chris replied. Then the fight was back on again. Chris and the warlock had each other by the throat, and both men began to squeeze. However, Chris knew that with the power of the triumvirate, he could kill Zachariah, and it felt so good. He unexpectedly pulled his hands away from Zachariah's neck, extracted his claws, and sliced the warlocks back and side open. Zachariah howled in pain as he let go of Chris' neck and fell to the ground.

Chris lowered himself to the ground, raised his hands, and unleashed his deadly blueish fire. Except, the fire wasn't blueish anymore but had turned into a deep dark red. Chris looked in surprise at the red rays of fire that shot from his hands.

"I'll kill you, you bastard," Zachariah screamed in frustration when the fire hit his arm. "Well, you can try," Chris said defiantly as he kept attacking. "Come and show me what you can do," Chris taunted the warlock while motioning with his hand for Zachariah to approach him.

The Warlock, however, turned to his two rogue Gods. "Don't stand there; attack the ranch, you idiots. Do I have to explain everything to you," he roared. Dhidysus and Leldur jumped and disappeared.

The earth began to shake more violently now than before as Chris and Zachariah clashed again. Chris seemed to get the upper hand because the warlock was bleeding profusely. Suddenly Chris had a huge sword that seemed to glow. He was about to push the sword into Zachariah's heart when the warlock jumped to his feet, grabbed Chris by the throat, and lifted him from the ground like he weighed nothing.

Chris grabbed Zachariah's hair and pulled his head back using so much force that he nearly tore the warlock's head from his torso. "Ready to die?" Chris growled as he prepared to break the warlock's neck. He had Zachariah in a death grip, from where there was no escape, not even for the mighty warlock because Chris was stronger.

Eric, Jory, James, and Max were watching anxiously, and they expected Chris to kill the warlock any minute. "Where did the sword come from?" Eric whispered. No one had an answer for the alpha. "Magic. Chris can conjure anything he wants or needs. It's a gift from Zeus."

Everyone turned to see Grace standing in the room. "How did you get here, sweetheart?" Max asked her daughter. "I'm not here, not really. Now I have to go because the two rogues started to attack the ranch, and we can't let that happen," Grace explained, then she was gone.

"I'm so confused right now," Max softly said. "I think that we all are a bit confused because so much has happened. It's a lot to comprehend," Jory said as he gently squeezed Max's shoulder. Then everyone focused on what was going on outside. Eric would never say it aloud, but he was fascinated seeing their children fight with deadly efficiency.

"Kill me; I don't care. I have my second in command who takes over. She will kill you," the warlock growled. "I don't know who she is, but let her try," Chris growled back. It was only a matter of minutes now before Chris would end Zachariah's life. "Oh, but you do know her very well, I might add," Zachariah was grinning now, even though he knew he was about to die. When Chris looked confused, the warlock said, evilly grinning, "I believe you know Alyssa? She's my second in command." Chris' world began to spin as he, without hesitation, broke Zachariah's neck. Then, to be absolutely sure, Chris decapitated the warlock. With one swift move, he severed Zachariah's head from his body.

Had he heard that correctly? Was Alyssa, his precious Alyssa Zachariah's right hand? Surely not. Zachariah was taunting him because he knew he was about to die. Too many emotions filled him that Chris couldn't take it. He still refused to believe that his precious girlfriend had betrayed him just like that. Chris had been convinced she loved him just as much as he loved her. Well, he would talk to her right now, ask her and force her to tell the truth.

Chapter Twenty Seven

Chris had disappeared Immediately after killing Zachariah. Carmen, Marcus, and Grace had captured Dhidysus and Leldur. The two rogues were now in the wasteland where they would stay for eternity. The hellhounds and the rest of the creatures had disappeared when Zachariah took his last breath.

At first, Eric and Jory thought that Chris had disappeared because he had to comprehend what had happened. Plus, it was the first time he had killed someone, even if it was a warlock, who threatened his family. However, it had been two days since Chris had disappeared. Jory suspected that this was something more than his son coming to terms with what had happened.

The alpha mate had tried to talk to Gaia about Chris' whereabouts and what had happened for his son to disappear without a word to his family. However, she had ignored his call until now. James and Max had gone home because all the excitement wasn't good for her unborn child. Grace and Marcus were traveling between the ranch and the Stanton Residence. They were worried about the safety of their parents, even though Zachariah was dead and his demise was confirmed by Chaos, who had praised The Four.

Eric and Jory were startled when Gaia appeared in their living room without letting them know. The earth shook, and Gaia looked worried. "What's going on? And, where is Chris?" Jory questioned. "That's why I'm here, to talk about your son," Mother Earth replied.

"Just, where is he? What happened that he disappeared?" Jory asked because he was worried sick. He knew that Chris was powerful and only a fool would attack him, but still. "Your son is about to destroy the earth because he was betrayed in the worst possible way," Gaia said. "Please, just explain what happened and tell us where Christopher is," Eric demanded.

Gaia frowned, but then she said, "His girlfriend, Alyssa Knight was Zachariah's right hand. We always thought it was Dhidysus or Leldur, but it turned out to be Alyssa. Zachariah set up the "Coincidental" meeting between her and Chris. He fell fast and hard for her." "Yes, we know. He even thought that she was the one," Eric interrupted, his voice barely human.

"Right now, he's looking for her, and if he finds Alyssa, he will end her existence. Chris is hurt beyond imagination, so much so that, in order to find her, he will destroy the earth if he has to. On top of that, Alyssa will continue Zachariah's work, which means she will come after you, and everyone who lives on the ranch," Gaia paused, and Jory knew that there was more bad news to come, and he wasn't wrong.

"Chris could lose control because Alyssa betrayed him. If that happens, we will have to intervene because we can't risk the earth being destroyed," Gaia said, and Jory saw the pain in her eyes. The alpha mate knew that Gaia had a weak spot for Chris. "You need to find him and bring him home, center him. Chris needs to unleash his rage but in a controlled environment. And, before you ask, no, I don't know where he is. He could be at Tartarus, trying to get information about Alyssa from the two rogues. But, on the other hand, she could have fled to a parallel world or even the demon realm. But it doesn't matter because Chris will find her eventually," Gaia said, and then she vanished.

"God damn!" Eric cursed. "Don't lose your focus, babe. We must concentrate on locating our boy before he causes irreversible damage," Jory said in a firm tone. The alpha mate was in daddy mode, which meant that he was calm and collected because he knew it was the only way to find their son. It would do no one any good if they let rage overtake them because then the focus was gone, and they would run around like a chicken without a head.

Eric glanced at Jory, and it broke the alpha mate's heart to see the devastation in Eric's eyes. "We will find him, I promise," Jory soothed if he only knew how.

******

"Tell me, where do I find this treacherous bitch?" Chris had Leldur by the throat as he slowly squeezed the life out of him. "I. I. I." It was all the rogue could muster because he couldn't breathe. Chris had entered the wasteland where he knew he would find Dhidysus and Leldur. Chris loosened his hold so Leldur could breathe again and thus talk.

"I'm asking for the last time; where do I find Alyssa," Chris growled. "I don't know; I swear I don't know. Please, don't hurt me anymore," Leldur began to beg. Chris knew that the rogue had spoken the truth, he slammed him against the rocks. "You disgust me," he said, then he was gone.

Chris sat on the cloud, watching the earth far beneath him. He thought of the ranch, his home, and how he missed his family. Chris shook his head because now was not the time; he needed to track down that godforsaken bitch and kill her slowly. He felt sick because he wasn't even sure if he would be able to end Alyssa's life. Could he kill the woman he had loved so much? Did he still love her? So many emotions passed, and the more he tried to comprehend, the more it confused him.

Had it all been a lie? How they had met, and the lovemaking, had that been an act? Chris' stomach cramped, and for a moment, he thought he had to throw up. What he needed was advice from his dad, but unfortunately, that wasn't possible. If he returned to the ranch, then they wouldn't let him leave. Chris shook his head again; what a fucking mess.

He didn't know how long he was gone in his search for Alyssa. It could have been hours; it could have been days, weeks, or even months. He didn't know and didn't care. "I trusted you, and I God damn loved you, and what did you do? You betrayed me; you fucking betrayed me, you bitch," Chris screamed.

After he killed Zachariah, Chris had orbed to Alyssa's apartment. He had been surprised that the apartment was empty. Now he knew that Zachariah had spoken the truth, which meant that Alyssa was on the run. However, Chris was determined to find her, and if he did, he would end her miserable existence. After checking Alyssa's apartment, Chris had entered the Tartarus, hoping that one of the two rogues knew where to find Alyssa.

Chris had called for Gaia, but she hadn't answered his call, and Chris knew he was alone. Would his parents help him? No, Chris didn't want to involve them, and the same was true for Carmen, Grace, and Marcus. Chris thought about his next move because there had to be a way to track down that treacherous excuse for a bitch.

"Hey," said a voice beside him, startling Chris. Without looking up, he said, "What do you want, Carmen." Chris didn't need to ask how she had found him because they were connected. He was also connected with Marcus and Grace, but not as tight as he was with his sister.

"Why don't you come home? Gaia told us what happened, and our dads want you home so they can help you through this difficult time," Carmen said softly. She didn't touch him because she knew that right now, Chris wouldn't appreciate that.

"I'm not returning before I found and killed that bitch," Chris growled. Carmen was about to say something, but Chris beat her to it. "Go home, and don't come after me anymore. Just leave me alone," he said, then he vanished. Carmen sighed; well, at least she'd tried.

Chris glanced around; he was in the parallel world, but which one? "Which one do you want it to be?" that was Alyssa's voice. Chris looked left and right but didn't see her. "You're not only a devious, treacherous bitch, but you're also a coward. Show yourself to face the consequences of what you did," Chris growled, but Alyssa didn't show and didn't say anything else. Rage, as he had never felt, surged through him as he vanished into another parallel world. This one was black and white, but Chris didn't seem to notice because his rage was about to consume him. His wolf was showing, but it wasn't his regular form; this one had something demonic over him.

Chris didn't know how long he had searched for her, but at least he was convinced she wasn't there and probably never had been. The rage got the better of him, and before he knew what he was doing, he entered the underworld. Hades would know where he could find Alyssa.

It didn't even occur that Hades wasn't particularly friendly with the pack; in fact, he hated Dacian, who was Chris' great-grandfather. Since Chris was consumed with rage, he didn't think clearly anymore, or else he would have never entered Hades' territory.

Chapter Twenty Eight

Chris materialized in Hades' portal, as they called it. Only a few could enter the underworld, and Chris was one of them. He looked up and yelled for Hades to show himself. "Why are you here? You must know that I hate intruders," Hades said as he appeared in front of Chris, legs apart and arms crossed over his chest.

Chris didn't care what Hades liked or didn't like; all he wanted was to know where he would find Alyssa. "Come with me," Hades said as he opened the door to his quarters with a wave of his hand. Chris followed; he wasn't scared because he could defend himself.

They sat down, and with a wave of his hand, Hades conjured milk and cookies. Chris frowned. "Are you for real?" he growled. Hades smiled. "What can I say? I love milk and cookies," he chuckled. "Tell me, what's your sin?" the ruler of the underworld inquired.

Chris felt like he had entered the world of Alice in Wonderland because this couldn't be real. Hades, drinking milk, and eating cookies? No way, not a great ruler as Hades.

Hades' eyes twinkled when he said, "I know what your sin is." "Oh, really? Well, enlighten me," Chris said. "You are a shifter or chimera because you harbor multiple spirits. Now Zeus pumped you full of unimaginable power, and I wonder why," Hades said.

Hades considered Chris for a long time before finally saying, "You need to return home and forget about Alyssa." Rage filled Chris again. "I won't rest until she's dead. No one, and I mean no one, betrays me and gets away with it." He glanced intently at Hades. "If you know where she is, then you better tell me," he said in a tone that told Hades that the man in front of him meant it. This was a man who wouldn't back down just because Hades told him to do so.

Hades looked thoughtful; he wanted to hate Chris like he hated Dacian and, because of that, the rest of the Wentworth Pack. However, he found that he actually liked the warrior who sat opposite him. Not only did he like him, but the man was damn attractive. Hades loved sex with women but didn't say no to handsome males either. Men like Chris weren't exactly his type because they were too masculine, too alpha.

When it came to having sex with another male, Hades always topped, and Chris didn't seem like a male who would play bottom. Then there was the question if Chris was gay because Hades had no clue. Apart from Dacian, the Wentworth Pack had never caught his interest, so he didn't really know its members. Well, he sure as hell would find out if Chris was into men or solely bedded women.

"Well?" a grim-sounding Chris said. Hades looked confused. "Well, what?" Chris sighed in irritation. "I asked you if you knew where I could find Alyssa," he said. Hades seemed to think about that, and his answer was careful. "Suppose I know, and if I tell you, what will you do?" he inquired. "Kill her," Chris answered without hesitation, making Hades sigh.

"There's a lot you don't know about Alyssa, and before I tell you her whereabouts, you need to know who she really is," Hades softly said. Chris felt sick because he had the feeling that more bad news about what he thought had been the love of his life was coming. And sure enough, he wasn't mistaken.

"By now, you must be aware that Alyssa isn't the person you think she is." Chris nodded because, yes, he knew that she was a two-timing treacherous bitch. "Aside from the fact that she betrayed you, you must know that she was Zachariah's partner, lover, whatever you want to call it. They were together for more than a hundred years, and she was deeply in love with good old Zach," Hades informed the shifter.

"Are you kidding me?" Chris growled as his eyes began to glow, and his body began to vibrate. "Calm down, handsome," Hades said, and Chris noticed a gentle command in the ruler's tone. However, he wasn't planning on calming down because this bitch had brought out the worst in him.

Hades stood and motioned for Chris to rise from the chair as well. "Give me your right hand," the ruler of the underworld softly demanded. Chris complied without hesitation, stunning himself. Next, Hades took Chris' hand and closed his eyes. Chris wanted to pull his hand back, but Hades' grip was too tight.

Hades glared at Chris, telling him without words to hold still, which Chris did. "Close your eyes," Hades said as he closed his eyes again. Chris didn't like it, but somehow he trusted Hades not to attack him while his eyes were closed.

It took a few minutes, but then Chris felt the rage slowly subside from his body. However, his heart was heavy, which wasn't so surprising. He had cared deeply for the woman, and when it concerned matters of the heart, one couldn't flip the switch and turn off the feelings.

"So," Hades said suddenly when he let go of Chris' hand, startling the shifter. "Now that we have your rage under control, I will tell you what you have to know about Alyssa," the ruler of the underworld softly said while eyeing him intently. Chris sank back in the chair again, waiting for Hades to share his shit about Alyssa.

"As I said, Alyssa was the love of Zachariah's life, and she adored him. That's why she agreed to make you fall in love with her. She had to lure you to a place where Zachariah had the upper hand. And, together, they planned to destroy you. Also, Alyssa is Felicia's child," Hades paused.

Chris felt the blood drain from his face. "Come again?" he said because had he heard that correctly? "Yep, she's Felicia's daughter. However, she thinks that her daughter died a long time ago. That she was murdered by one of the Gods for betraying them. Even then, she couldn't be trusted," Hades added.

"So, my Aunt doesn't know her daughter is still alive? That I dated her?" Chris growled. Hades nodded. Well, technically, Felicia wasn't blood-related; she was one of the three angels who were banned from heaven. Dacian had created them, and even though he called them his children, they weren't his by blood. Chris knew all this. However, Finn was Chris' grandfather by blood because he and Annabella were Jory's biological parents.

Chris was getting madder by the minute. He adored Felicia, and she would be devastated when she found out that her daughter was still alive. And that she had become one of the pack's biggest enemies because she had teamed up with Zachariah. Chris wondered if she would come after him because he had killed Zachariah. If she truly had adored that murderous monster, the chance she would come for him was very real.

"So, Alyssa is aware that her mother thinks she's dead?" "Yes." Then another question came to mind; Chris hoped that the ruler of the underworld knew the answer to this question. Hades considered the man who sat opposite him for a long time. "I'm sorry to say, but Alyssa is very much aware of that fact. I know that she hated Felicia. However, I do not know why."

"I assume she went over to the dark side, just like Zachariah?" Chris questioned. It dawned on him that it didn't hurt much anymore to talk and hear about Alyssa and what she really was. Had that been Hades' doing?

"You feel what you feel; I hate to admit it, but I don't have any influence on that. Well, not with you anyway, because you're too powerful. It almost looks like Zeus gave you an overdose of magic and power," Hades said. They talked for a while longer, and Chris saw, to his astonishment, that Hades ate the cookies and drank the milk. So, he hadn't been joking about that, which was interesting.

Chris sighed and looked troubled as he said, "I guess I have to tell Felicia." Hades nodded. "I guess so," he replied, and to Chris' astonishment, the ruler of the underworld's expression was a sad one, which was interesting. Hades stood and moved toward Chris; their eyes met. "You need to go home, really, you should. I guess Alyssa will come for you, and she will come to the ranch first because she expects you to be there." Hades' smile was rueful when he added, "If the situation wasn't so dire, then."

Chris frowned because what the hell? But, before he could respond, Hades waved with his hand, and Chris was transported back to the ranch. Chris blinked a few times and saw his family staring at him; he was home.

Chapter Twenty Nine

"What happened just now?" Eric said after Chris had materialized in the living room where his family had gathered. Chris looked as confused as he felt. His father almost seemed hostile; why would that be?

Jory let his hand rest on Eric's arm, calming his mate, whose anger was evident. "Why are you so angry? Is it because I went in search of that treacherous bitch that wants to see us dead?" a still flabbergasted Chris questioned, but he didn't look at Eric; instead, he eyed Jory.

"You were away for nearly a week without so much as letting us know that you're alright. You could have been dead, and we wouldn't have known," Eric growled as his anger rose even more. "Baby? What's going on?" Jory asked because this was not how the alpha normally behaved. Eric had never been aggressive toward anyone in the pack, let alone against one of his children.

"He's possessed. We need to contain him before he does something he'll regret later," Cassandra whispered, hoping that Eric hadn't heard her. But, unfortunately, she was wrong because the alpha had heard every word. "You want to restrain me? Me, alpha of the Wentworth Pack?" he growled as his eyes began to change color.

"Alyssa," Chris growled as he motioned for Cassandra and Annabella to do their magic and try to restrain Eric. "It Must be Alyssa's doing," Chris said. "Oh hell," Jake whispered as Eric began to grow, which meant that he would shift into one of his monstrous and very deadly forms.

Chris closed his eyes and focussed on Alyssa while the angels aided the two witches and Dacian. If he only could stop Alyssa from influencing his father. *What do you want? When I'm finished with your daddies, I'll come for you. But, first, I want you to witness the pack's demise,* Alyssa's voice violently invaded Chris' mind, making him double back in agony. "Hurry, because Alyssa is preparing to kill him," Chris managed to croak before he lost consciousness.

Jory didn't have another choice but to intervene, with Chris down and Eric on the verge of losing control. He rose from the chair he was sitting in while Cassandra and Annabella tried to contain Eric with their most powerful spells. The alpha mate stretched his arms and pointed at his mate. "Babe, I'm so sorry. Believe me; this is going to hurt me more than it will you," he murmured.

Jory was very powerful because they were mates. And, because the bond between them was extremely powerful, he was probably the only one who would succeed in restraining the alpha. He was using a mix of a powerful spell and his own magic to prevent Eric from becoming a rogue. Jory didn't know how, but he knew this was Alyssa's plan. She wanted Eric to go rogue, and when that happened, there was no way back. Jory would die before he let anything happen to his precious mate.

"Get away from him, now!" Jory commanded, his voice raised so they would hear him. Annabella and Cassandra reacted fast and stepped back from the alpha as Jory unleashed his fire. However, this time it wasn't the deadly blueish fire. Instead, the fire he unleashed was a light orange, which was Jory's favorite color. The fire engulfed Eric, who began to roar in a fury.

May the fire restrain you. May the fire keep you safe

My protection is your shield

My protection is your support

My worries will give you strength and protect you from harm

Keep the evil at bay

Evil curse, you can't stay

My blood is red, my soul is true

I take this evil and send it back to you

Jory had to repeat the spell three more times before Eric gained control and his massive form changed into a human again. The pack and its extended members had watched with bated breath at Jory and how he had conjured his magic to save the alpha.

After Jory redrew the fire and stopped repeating the spell, he saw that Eric was lying on the floor and had lost consciousness, just like their son. "That was." Annabella didn't know what to say because she was too stunned. "That's our boy," Cassandra whispered, and her expression said it all. The witch was very proud of her grandson.

Jory knelt beside Eric and gently stroked the unruly curls out of his face. "Wake up, my love. You need to wake up because we need you," Jory kept whispering. The alpha mate looked up when he felt Chris stir. His son's aura had been good, so Jory knew Chris wasn't in imminent danger. Because of that, he had been able to focus entirely on Eric.

Jory didn't want to think if things had been different because if he had to divide his focus between his son and his mate, the outcome would have been different. Jory knew he was very powerful, but he doubted if he could have saved both his son and mate.

The alpha mate turned to his son. "How are you feeling? What happened?" He asked. Jory could only guess that it was because of Alyssa. Chris had been madly in love with her, and she had betrayed him in the worst conceivable way.

"We wait until your father regains consciousness, and then you will inform us about everything that happened and why you left so abruptly." Jory requested water for himself and Chris, and a moment later, Jake handed him two bottles. "Can I get some too?" said a voice from beside Jory.

"Eric, babe. Thank God you're awake. How are you feeling," Jory asked while he handed Eric his bottle of water. "What the hell happened?" Eric growled as he suddenly grabbed his head with both hands and began to groan. "Eric? Eric?" When the alpha mate didn't get a response, he reacted immediately. Jory put his hands over Eric's and pushed healing powers into the alpha's head.

Jory had to give a lot because he felt how much he had drained himself. Eric took too much of his energy, which wasn't good. "Mom? Help me," Jory whispered when he couldn't disconnect his magic from Eric. It seemed that the alpha held on to his mate with all his might, which really wasn't good.

His grandmother, Cassandra, and his mother, Annabella, were at his side in a second. "He's draining me. I need to sever the magical thread," Jory managed to say.

The witches went to work without further questioning. They held hands and started chanting something Jory couldn't decipher. What seemed like hours, but probably only took minutes before Jory felt the thread being severed, and he could breathe again.

Eric looked dazed like he didn't know what just had happened. "Baby, are you alright?" the alpha inquired. Jory shook his head because no, he wasn't. His mate had drained him to the point that it became dangerous. "Here, drink this," Annabella said as she handed him a glass with blueish liquid in it.

"I knew that you're good, but damn I didn't know you were this fast with brewing a potion," Jory said as he took the glass and brought it to his lips. "Aw, it's a sports drink," he chuckled after emptying the glass. "Yes, I'm good, but even I can't manage to brew something within a few minutes," Annabella laughed.

An hour later, Chris began to explain what exactly had happened, what Zachariah had told him, and how betrayed he had felt. Jory and Eric could feel the rage boiling inside Annabella and Cassandra. As a true alpha, Eric had the power to calm pack members when they were about to lose control because they got scared or, in this case, very angry.

Jory watched in awe when the people in the room began to relax. However, Cassandra and Annabella needed a bit more time, and Eric was now solely focusing on the two women. At first, the two witches didn't seem affected by the soothing power Eric let loose in the room.

However, when the alpha pushed more power into the two women, they finally reacted.

"Thank you," Cassandra said as she smiled ruefully at Eric. "Yes, thank you, Eric. I guess we lost a bit of control," Annabella said. The alpha smiled warmly; he wasn't angry because how could he? Cassandra and Annabella had been furious on Chris' behalf.

"We need to find her as soon as possible. Who knows what she's capable of? Apparently, Zachariah's demise hit her hard," Jory looked apologetically at his son. "I know, and I have to live with the knowledge that she didn't love me," Chris softly replied. "I'm truly sorry, son," Eric whispered. Chris didn't respond because what could he say?

Alyssa had played him like a pro, and he had fallen for it, big time. Chris wanted to say he wouldn't let that happen again, but he knew he had to continue believing in love. He heard stories of humans who had their hearts broken, again and again. Chris only hoped that he never had to experience a broken heart again. It hurt like a bitch, and somewhere deep inside him, he still loved her. However, he knew that when he found Alyssa, he would have to kill her because she wouldn't stop to come after his family. And no one hurt his family and got away with it.

Chris might still have feelings for Alyssa, which was expected because when it concerned matters of the heart, there wasn't a switch to turn off someone's feelings. But Chris was sure that he was able to end her existence when he got his hands on her.

Chapter Thirty

A week had passed, and still no sign of Alyssa. Chris was thinking of heading out to the underworld again to see if she had shown up there. Unfortunately, the underworld was one of the few places Chris couldn't sense her. This past week, he had tried to track Alyssa down and almost succeeded twice. However, it seemed she was always two steps ahead of him, which enraged Chris even more.

So, now he had to find a way to contact Hades because he didn't want to enter the underworld again without the ruler's permission. Even though Chris was very powerful, he didn't want to anger Hades. When he'd entered the underworld the last time, Hades had told him not to enter without his permission again. Chris hadn't thought rationally when he'd entered. He had been so full of rage. "Next time, I won't be so forgiving." Hades had said, and Chris had understood. It was all about respect.

"Dinner is ready." "Just a sec," Chris answered absentmindedly. Jory watched Chris from the other side of the room, and it killed him that he wasn't able to help him. These past days, Chris had redrawn more and more. Eric and Jory were at a loss for how to help their son. It seemed that at this moment, Carmen the only one was who could get through to Chris. He had even blocked Marcus and Grace from his mind. Jory could only hope that his son hadn't completely severed the ties with Marcus and Grace.

Chris had told Carmen that The Four didn't need to exist anymore now that Zachariah was dead. Carmen had other ideas, but Chris didn't want to hear about them. He had turned his back to her and basically had dismissed his sister.

"I need to contact Hades," Chris said while standing with his back to Jory. "Then we will find a way to make that happen. But, first, you really need to eat; otherwise, it will weaken you, and you need your strength," Jory sounded calm, and his tone was soothing.

"Emma made your favorite dish, quinoa burger with mashed potatoes and a mixed salad. The salad has even mushrooms in it," Jory said, smiling. Chris turned. "Well, I can't say no to that now, can I?" he softly replied, then they walked toward the dining room. Eric and Jory had added several rooms to the main house, and one of them was a spacious dining room, which had room for everyone. Since Jory had joined the pack, others had followed, and the pack had extended immensely with the addition of angels, an archangel, and even the God of War because he was Emma Wentworth's, destined mate. Then there was Jory's grandmother and mother, two powerful witches.

When Chris stepped into the room, he saw that everyone was present. Marcus sat to Carmen's left and Grace to her right. Dacian had an animated conversation with Jake. Max and James were present as well, and she was showing. Just a couple of months and, she would give birth to a baby girl.

Emma looked up and smiled brightly when she saw Chris standing in the room. "Finally, I was afraid you would let your food get cold," she chuckled. "Come, sit," she said as she patted the seat of the empty chair beside her.

Chris looked at Jory and then walked around the table and sat beside Emma. Caitlin, Rose and Alex's daughter, sat in her high chair and refused every spoon full of food to the point where she tried to knock the spoon out of Rose's hands. However, Rose apparently had expected it and redrew the spoon just in time, so Caitlin missed. The girl eyed her father, and then she started crying. Rose looked apologetically at Eric. "I'm sorry, but it seems that lately, Caitlin hates food," she said.

"Well, why don't you give her the spoon and let her deal with it on her own? She's nearly six months now," Eric gently suggested. Rose considered him for a few seconds, smiled, and handed Caitlin the spoon. The girl stopped crying and giggled as she took the spoon and started eating. Well, she tried anyway; a lot of food fell to the floor, much to Sage and Chloe's delight. Molly and Dudley stayed on the blanket beside the fireplace.

Dinner was enjoyable, with everyone chatting with the one who sat next to them. Chris noticed just how much he'd missed these gatherings. These days it wasn't often that everyone was present for dinner. It seemed like a normal, cozy dinner where everyone would have fun if it hadn't been for Alyssa.

"Everything alright?" Jory asked quietly. Chris nodded; "Yeah, fine. I only." He stopped mid-sentence, and Jory understood. His son still had feelings for Alyssa, and he hated himself for it. "It's expected that you still have feelings for her. Don't beat yourself up because it doesn't help. Accept what is and deal with what comes your way."

There was so much Jory wanted to ask, needed to know, but he didn't have the heart because Alyssa still was a sore point. He was desperate to know if his son was indeed able to end Alyssa's life. It was what worried the alpha mate and kept him up at night. Because if Chris would hesitate, then Alyssa would kill him for sure. The thought made Jory shudder. Then there was that encounter Chris had with Hades, the ruler of the underworld. Hades hadn't attacked Chris; on the contrary, they had sat down and talked about Chris' problem.

It seemed that no one wanted to leave early because when dinner was finished, everyone stayed seated. Armand, JJ, and Finn cleared the table, did the dishes, and cleaned the kitchen. After all, Emma, Rose, and Annabella had cooked a fabulous dinner, then it was a given that others cleared the table and did the dishes.

"Are you still searching for me, my love?" Alyssa's voice reared through Chris' mind again, but this time, he didn't even flinch, which seemed to set off the woman even more. *"I'm two steps ahead of you, moron. You will never find me, if you do, I'll be ready, and I will end your life."* Her soothing voice had changed into a screaming; this time, he grabbed his head because the pain was unbearable.

The room had gone very quiet, and everyone was staring at Chris, who was on his knees. "That bad, uh?" Dacian said. Chris eyed the archangel in confusion; did he know what just had happened? "I know what just happened, and I also know how painful it can be," Dacian softly said. "Follow me, please," he said as he moved toward the sliding doors that led onto the back deck. Chris cocked his head but didn't protest as he stood and followed the archangel outside.

Dacian stopped at the railing that prevented one from falling off the terras. The archangel turned and eyed Chris for a minute, then said, "I can teach you how to protect yourself from these attacks on your brain. If you're interested, that is." Chris was very interested because, more than anything, he wanted to be able to close his mind. Because if Alyssa could penetrate his mind, then others would probably be able to do the same, and that wasn't an option. When Alyssa had invaded his mind, Chris had felt vulnerable, and it was something he didn't like. He didn't want to admit it, but Alyssa had made him feel weak. Right now, Chris doubted if he would be able to catch her because, God damn, that bitch was clever.

"Yes, I want to learn how to close my mind. So, if you could teach me, that would be great," Chris replied. "Alright, we will start now because the sooner you learn how to block your mind, the better. Follow me," Dacian walked to the back of the garden straight to the orchard.

Two hours later, Chris and Dacian stepped into the living room again. "How did it go?" Eric asked quietly. Chris' smile was rueful; he said, "It takes more energy than I thought." He eyed his dads because Jory had joined them. "I need a shower," he added before heading for the stairs.

Dacian eyed Jory and Eric. "He's not doing so great. Chris is suffering from the betrayal of Alyssa. When he's able to close his mind and shut her out, it will be a step in the right direction. But you need to be aware that, at this moment, he's still in love with her, and he hates himself for that," the archangel explained calmly.

"I want Alyssa dead because not only is she a threat to the pack, but even more to Chris because of what he feels for her," Jory growled, and the expression on the alpha mate's face said it all. He was furious, and rightly so because this concerned his son, and Jory would protect Chris with all his might.

"Now I understand why she didn't want to meet us," Jory continued. Eric and Dacian looked expectantly at the alpha mate. "She must have been aware that I can see people for what they are. I can see their aura, and if necessary, I can see right into their soul. I'm sure if I would have met Alyssa, she would have raised red flags," Jory said, looking at Eric and Dacian for their opinion.

Chapter Thirty One

Another week had passed, and Chris had learned to close his mind and block Alyssa. She had tried to enter Chris' mind on several occasions but failed every time. And that enraged her to the point that she threatened to come to the ranch and slaughter everyone. That resulted that the pack being on high alert.

Gaia had opened her home for Rose, Alex, and their young daughter. Because Max was pregnant, she had been welcome to. The others were ready to defend their home. Chris wondered who would fight at her side because even though she was powerful, she couldn't attack the ranch on her own. Zachariah, who had been Alyssa's lover, was dead, so who would she turn to?

Alyssa had declared war, and Chris knew she would come with the intention to kill them all. Well, they would be ready; let her try. The thought of Rose, her mate, who was human, and their young child fleeing from the ranch, had enraged him beyond boiling point.

Chris had also noticed that the feelings he had for Alyssa were gone; he detested her for everything she stood for. How could someone be so vindictive? Zachariah had deserved to be killed; why didn't Alyssa know that? How could she ignore the fact that Zachariah had been a psychopath? He sighed and hoped the attack would come sooner rather than later because he wanted everyone safe. Chris wanted the pack to live in peace; he wanted Rose and her family back at the ranch. He wanted Max safe so that she could enjoy her pregnancy. Yep, Chris wanted a lot, but he knew that it was only possible if he would kill Alyssa.

Chris dressed and descended the stairs. Today he would go horseback riding with Dorian, his father's second in command. Chris longed for alone time, but right now, it simply was too dangerous. When he entered the barn, Dorian saddled his horse while Chris walked over to the stall where Beau stood, patiently waiting.

Suddenly Chris stiffened; something was terribly wrong. "What is it?" Dorian questioned. "She's here; I can sense her," Chris whispered as he rushed back to the house, Dorian hot on his heels.

"We need everyone back at the house, Alyssa is on her way, and she will soon be here. And, I sense that she's not alone." Eric mentally sent out a demand to the pack to come to the main house immediately. "Can you sense how many are with her?" Chris eyed his dad, his expression grim when he said, "She has an army with her." He didn't know what that army consisted of, but they would be deadly.

Chris reared back and slammed against the wall when a force so powerful hit him full in his chest. "Chris," Jory screamed in pure panic as he rushed to his son's side. "What happened?" the alpha mate asked as he knelt beside his son.

Chris smiled as he stood, "The triumvirate. This time, they hit me with so much more power. I can taste it," he explained. Jory looked thoughtful; he said, "Well, that could mean you will need it. That Alyssa's army will be forceful." "I guess so, but let her come. I'll deal with her my way, and if necessary, I will kill her," Chris replied, and Jory heard the determination in his son's voice.

"You still don't know what army she brings with her?" Eric questioned. Chris shook his head because he had no clue. "I don't know, but whatever she brings will be powerful. Otherwise, the triumvirate wouldn't have been activated. They gave me more power to even out the balance," Chris answered while he kept staring out of the window.

"We're ready for her," Dorian said. Chris smiled, but it didn't reach his eyes. Then, the ground began to shake. Chris eyed the people in the room; he said, "She's here."

Annabella and Cassandra had reinforced the windows and doors with wards and powerful spells. They even used potions to strengthen the spells. JJ and Armand had brought the few horses who still were at the ranch to a neighboring farm. A feline shifter owned this farm, so he had understood when Eric had explained the situation.

Emma gasped when trees were pushed to the ground, roots and all. "What the hell is that?" Jory whispered when he saw, well, he wasn't sure of what he saw. "Dear God," JJ whispered as he saw hellhounds, and all had two heads. "What the hell? How did she get these monsters?" Chris mumbled as his blood began to boil.

The thought of someone in his family falling victim to one of these monsters was unbearable. Jory's eyes grew huge as he saw his son sprouting hairs. Thick blond hairs, not like a common shifter. Chris began to grow; he was nearly eight feet of pure muscle. Finally, Alyssa came into sight, and Chris roared in a fury, making everyone cover their ears.

Chris looked at his two dads; then he was gone; it happened so fast that no one, not even Eric, had seen him move. Jory let out a battle cry, and then everyone rushed outside. Some had changed into their wolf, and some were fighting while staying in human form. Dacian was waving with his hands, and deadly fire hit the beasts one after another. Dacian smiled in satisfaction when the beasts from hell went down, howling in rage and pain.

Jory was fighting with three hell beasts; he hit one with his deadly blue fire, which turned to orange and then to a dark red. The first beast that was hit didn't go down like the ones that got hit by Dacian's fire. The beast that was hit by Jory's fire exploded. The pack was fighting for their lives, and neither Jory nor Eric had time to see where Chris was.

Two beasts attacked JJ, and he managed to take one down, but the other one jumped on JJ's back, making him howl in pain. Armand was at JJ's side in seconds, grabbed the beast, and tore both its heads from its torso.

JJ was lying motionless on the ground, blood pouring out of the wound that was inflicted by the beast. Armand cursed as he lifted Jordan into his arms and orbed them away from the battlefield.

Eric had shifted into his second form, which meant that he was on two legs, nearly eight feet tall, with long arms and exceptionally long deadly talons. Jory took a second to take in the beauty of his mate and noticed that Eric's claws were more extended than he had ever seen them.

Jory had been distracted for a little too long, and the sudden pain in his back made him focus on fighting again. He turned, let himself fall on his back, and managed to throw the beast off him. However, not before the monster had sliced his back open.

Jory was bleeding profoundly, and he began to feel weak. Then the next beast attacked him, and Jory had great difficulty defending himself. Dacian, who apparently had seen his grandson in trouble, rushed to his side. Jory's fire wasn't as powerful as it should be, and the monster didn't even stop. However, Dacian's fire was as deadly as ever, and he managed to burn and kill the beast that had attacked his grandson.

Dacian lifted Jory into his arms and orbed him to the safety of the main house, which still had successfully repulsed all attacks. *"Baby? What's going on?"* Eric asked through their mind link. *"I'm safe,"* Jory panted, and that was all Eric needed to know. Dacian lowered Jory onto the couch, and Sarah already had her medical things ready.

Eric, a true alpha was very powerful, as was Jory and the angels and Ares; however, their enemies were as well. That made the fight intense, and it looked like it was on the verge of becoming a battle of exhaustion. They had been fighting for many hours, and it didn't seem to end soon. Every time they killed the monsters from hell, new ones appeared.

Carmen, Marcus, and Grace were fighting like pros, and Grace even killed a two-headed dog when the three attacked Billy.

Chapter Thirty Two

"Catch me if you can," Alyssa snapped right before she disappeared. Chris didn't need time to react, as he, too, vanished. "NO," Eric screamed as he saw his son and Alyssa vanish before his eyes.

Chris didn't know where he was going; he was simply following Alyssa's trace. However, when she materialized in a cave, Chris was right behind her and immediately grabbed her by the hair. "Oh, just the way I like it," she panted. "Are you kidding me?" Chris was stunned because this was a totally different woman than the Alyssa he'd come to know and love.

How had it been possible to fool him like this? Chris always prided himself as someone who could read people perfectly. Well, in this case, Alyssa had done an excellent job of fooling him. Chris had fallen so fast and so hard for her, which wasn't like him at all. Then a thought occurred, could it have been possible that they put him under some kind of spell?

He dismissed that thought just as fast as it had come. He might have fallen for Alyssa's lies, but no one should be able to put him under a spell, right? Alyssa's voice made him grab her hair even tighter. Alyssa seemed to enjoy Chris being rough. "I know you were good, but." She didn't get the chance to finish because Chris pushed her away from him, raised his hands, and unleashed blueish fire. It was the same fire as his dad's.

Alyssa, however, deflected the fire with ease, stunning Chris. "Is that all you got?" she taunted. Chris didn't reply because he knew she wanted to distract him so she could attack. Then Alyssa conjured a sword and charged. Chris was just in time to jump aside to avoid being sliced open. She handled the sword with practiced ease, letting Chris know it wasn't the first time she had used the damn thing.

Even though it had surprised him, he didn't show it. "You can do better than that," he growled despite her seeming to be one with the sword. "I hate you so much, and I will dance on your dead body after I kill you," she said, voice low and deadly. "You can try, bitch," Chris replied, and then the fight was on. Alyssa charged again, trying to decapitate Chris, who was faster and dodged her with practiced ease.

"They taught you well during the aging process," she said, meaning Chris' fighting skills. "No, this is who I am," Chris responded. Alyssa cocked her head like she was confused by his answer. "No, this can't be you," she said as she charged again. "Oh, but it is me. And I killed Zachariah, and I will end your miserable existence too because you don't deserve to live," Chris growled while he dodged her attacks again.

She kept coming at him, but she wasn't able to slice him with her sword, which seemed to make her insecure, make her hesitate, for just a second. That one second of hesitation was enough for Chris to slam her into the wall. "So, you do hit girls. Zachariah told me you didn't have it in you," Alyssa chuckled. "Are you getting a kick out of men who abuse you?" Chris exclaimed because who would like that?

"I like it rough," she replied with a nasty smile, which should have given Chris the willies, but somehow it didn't. "Come on, hit me, show me that you're a big boy," Alyssa taunted as she moved toward him. Chris was thrown off kilter by her behavior. He didn't understand what was happening; hell, he didn't even know where he was. He had followed Alyssa without thinking things through.

"And, for the record, I don't hit women. But since I don't see you as a woman, I don't mind fighting with you because you are." Chris paused because he didn't know what she was or how to categorize her. She definitely didn't qualify as a woman, in his opinion. Was she a demon? "Are you a demon?" Chris had to ask. Alyssa laughed. "You noticed just now, I'm hurt," she laughed even harder.

"I came to Zachariah in a dream, and he fell in love with me. He wanted me with him all the time, so he used dark magic to give me a solid form." "You're a succubus?" Chris whispered. "He and I were together for many centuries, and you killed him, and for that, you will pay," Alyssa screamed suddenly, and then she attacked Chris again. This time, she used martial arts as she kicked Chris in the stomach. Chris reeled back but recovered immediately. Alyssa attacked again, and this time he was prepared and blocked the attack.

Now it was Chris' turn; with the speed of light, he grabbed her and threw her with so much force against the wall that the cave began to shake.

Alyssa shook her head and looked dazed; it looked like she wanted to say something but couldn't find the words. Chris took the opportunity to move in for the kill. He took the sword that Alyssa had dropped, swung it through the air, and severed Alyssa's head from her torso in one swift move. She didn't even scream because it had happened so fast.

Chris collapsed as he gasped for air. He glanced over to Alyssa's headless body and shook his head. This was so not how he had imagined his relationship to end. He didn't even notice that his body still was vibrating with energy until he heard rumbling, then the earth began to shake.

Chris had used so much force when he slammed Alyssa against the wall that the cave was about to collapse. Chris knew that he needed to get out of there fast. So he didn't hesitate but orbed right back to the ranch. But unfortunately, he didn't have time to take Alyssa's body with him.

Chris materialized right into the battle that still was going on. Still upset because he killed Alyssa, Chris wasn't in the mood. He glanced around and frowned when he didn't see Jory. The fighting continued as Chris went into the house and saw that his dad was wounded. Something inside him snapped when he saw his dad lying on the couch, blood still gushing from his wounds.

Something broke inside him, and suddenly Chris had enough of the fight and hatred; it all had to stop, right this moment. He was determined to bring peace to his family; if he had to destroy half the earth to end the battle, he would. Sarah, who was tending Jory's wounds, and Dacian and Finn, who were guarding, looked stunned when he materialized. Chris didn't say a word as he stormed outside. He looked up to the sky and raised his hands as if he wanted to rip the clouds apart. "ENOUGH," he screamed. Making everyone cover their ears, everyone, except the two-headed dogs, the ones who didn't disappear fast enough, exploded. The silence that followed was deafening.

Chris was vibrating with rage because he was fed up with the fighting, the blood, the threats, and the fear that had his family in its grip for too long now. Zachariah had even gone so far as to send his lover to seduce him, in which she had succeeded.

That bastard had almost managed to get the upper hand, but for Chris, his family had been more important than Alyssa. It had been Zachariah's goal to make Chris fall in love with Alyssa so much that he would choose her above his family. Well, that hadn't happened.

The fight with Alyssa hadn't really been much, but Chris was still reeling at the thought of decapitating her, which wasn't that strange. He had been very much in love with her. Now he had killed his ex-lover, whom he still had feelings for.

******

"It's okay, you know," Jory said. Chris stood in front of the large floor-to-ceiling windows, staring into the night. Jory sighed because he didn't know how to reach his son. A week had passed since Chris had ended the battle by throwing all of his power into the fight. It had drained Chris to the point of passing out for a couple of hours.

Jory had expected his son to be mourning his ex-lover because he really had loved that woman. However, that Chris had spiraled into what seemed a depression had stunned him. Maybe he had loved her more than the alpha mate had anticipated. Whatever it was, Jory wanted his son happy again if he only knew how.

"I'll be in the sitting room if you need me," he said. When Chris didn't respond, Jory turned and left because what else could he do? "Hey, baby? How is he?" Eric asked as he pulled Jory close. Eric and Jory took turns trying to reach their son in any way possible, but neither had been successful.

Chris had distanced himself from his family, which wasn't good. Not only would it make him vulnerable, but he suffered mentally, too. That Jory wasn't able to reach his son was hurting the alpha mate more than he had anticipated. He knew that Eric was worried too. What a fucking mess.

Jory inhaled deeply, trying to calm himself because if he would lose control, it would signal disaster. The alpha mate lifted his head; their eyes met, and it worried Eric to see so much pain in his mate's beautiful peepers.

"Our son will be okay; he just needs time to comprehend and accept that he was fooled by Alyssa. I still can't believe that she was a succubus. No wonder Chris fell for her," Eric whispered in Jory's hair. Jory leaned heavily into Eric's strong and comforting body. "I hope so," he whispered. "He will," Eric said, and he prayed he was right.

A succubus had touched Chris, and there was no telling if their son would ever get over Alyssa. "It would have been much easier if she had been human," Jory said. "I know, baby. But, we will be there for him every step of the way," Eric said.

They stood holding each other for a long time. The alpha and his mate were worried because no one knew what kind of influence the succubus had on Chris. Jory was glad she was dead so that she couldn't come after Chris anymore.

Usually, when a succubus had set her eyes on someone, that person would never be able to free himself from her. When she was done with her victim, she killed them. So, yes, Jory, Eric, and the rest of their family were glad she was dead.

No one had ever been able to resist a succubus, and that Chris had not only refused her but killed her said something about his strength and determination. However, he was suffering from the loss, and the alpha and alpha mate knew it would take time for Chris to heal.

Eric and Jory looked up when they heard someone entering the room; it was Finn. "Remember that Chris resisted her, and that counts for something. So we need to trust him because that's what he needs right now, our love, and our trust that if he needs help, he will ask for it," said Finn. Eric nodded, Finn was a fallen angel and Jory's father, and Eric respected that. It was the reason that he was allowed to interfere and give his opinion.

Chapter Thirty Three

"Any idea where our son is?" Eric asked his mate. Jory shook his head because he hadn't seen Chris in days. "No, but he's alright," Jory paused, then added, "I would feel it if he wasn't." Eric stood behind Jory and wrapped his arms around his waist. "Even so, it doesn't feel good. He should be home with his family to help him cope with what happened," the alpha said.

"I know, but Chris seems to think otherwise. So as much as I want him home, it's up to Chris," Jory softly said. Eric felt so much sadness coming from his mate, and he didn't want to, but it made him angry. "It's time that he comes home to face reality," Eric said, and the alpha didn't sound too pleased.

Since he ended the battle, Chris had retreated from his family emotionally. However, Eric had been grateful that Jory still had some kind of link with their son. To say that Chris had been upset after Alyssa's betrayal was an understatement. He had disappeared some time ago, and no one knew his whereabouts.

Dacian had offered to search for Chris, but Jory had told him not to. So it really was up to Chris to return home to his family.

"Hello," Rose softly greeted as she strode into the room, making Eric and Jory turn. The alpha mate smiled brightly when he saw Caitlin, who stretched her little chubby arms. "Oh, little princes, come to Uncle Jory," the alpha mate cooed as he took the baby from Rose.

Eric nodded his approval because the absence of Chris had a significant impact on the alpha mate. Jory didn't smile that often anymore. Seeing the radiant smile on his mate's face made Eric feel good. He had used the link between him and the pack and asked Rose to join them, bringing Caitlin. The alpha knew it would cheer up his mate, and he was right, seeing the joy in Jory's eyes.

Suddenly Eric lifted his head; he was listening. Then Jory looked up, and his expression became guarded. "He's home. Our boy is home," the alpha mate whispered. Rose looked from one to the other, and neither made a move to leave the room.

Rose took Caitlin from Jory and quietly left the room. "Are you ready?" Eric softly questioned. "I don't know, but I guess I don't have a choice," Jory replied. Eric didn't respond because he knew Jory had suffered when Chris disappeared without a word.

Chris stood in the hall, and Jory barely recognized his son. His hair was long; he even had a beard. For a moment, Eric, Jory, and Chris stood motionless, then Jory smiled and spread his arms wide. "Come here," he softly said, and Chris didn't need a second invitation as he rushed into his dad's arms.

"Welcome home, son," Jory whispered as he nearly crushed Chris. After Jory finally let go, Eric took over. He, too, hugged the living daylights out of his son. "You must be hungry," Jory said as he headed to the kitchen, Eric and Chris hot on his heels. It was what Jory always did when he was stressed, nervous, or, in this case, thrown off kilter; he went into the kitchen and prepared food. Chris returning home was the last thing he'd expected. The alpha mate had hoped and prayed for his son to come home, but he really hadn't expected it.

"Sit and spill it," Jory said as he pointed his spatula to the table. Chris looked at Eric; then he sat down. Eric offered to help Jory prepare food, which the alpha mate declined. Jory needed to focus on making sandwiches. Chris' eyes lit up when he saw the sandwiches that had scrambled eggs on them. "My favorite. Thank you, dad," he softly said.

Jory saw the relief on Chris' face; had he expected they would be mad at him? "Your father and I are so glad that you're home again. But, you need to talk to us, don't shut us out. And, where did you go, and why did you stay away for so long?" Jory questioned as he put the plate filled with sandwiches on the table.

Chris sighed because this was so difficult. He took a bite of his sandwich and eyed his dads. He wasn't sure if he should tell them where he had been and why. However, Chris knew he didn't have a choice because he had put his family through hell by disappearing as he did.

"I asked Gaia to help me process everything that happened after the aging. I didn't understand why I was so sensitive and depressed after Alyssa's betrayal. It's not who I am. Okay, what Alyssa did was unexpected, and I was hurt by it, but it shouldn't have affected me like that. Gaia explained that something had gone wrong during the aging process and that someone had invaded my brain. Which, of course, I already knew. However, what I didn't know was that this person had planted doubt and sensitivity to weaken me," Chris paused.

"I don't understand. Did someone mess with your brain?" Jory whispered because he was shocked. Then he narrowed his eyes and asked in a low and menacing tone, "Do you know who it was?" Chris shrugged; it was something that he still had to find out. Gaia didn't have a clue either, which was strange. Someone as powerful as Mother Earth should be able to find the bastard who had tampered with Chris' mind. As it was, she hadn't known, but she had helped Chris get rid of the self-pity, doubts, and depression by searching and removing the tiny seed that was planted into Chris' brain.

Jory gasped, and then he began to glow. It was a faint light blue color at first, but then it rapidly changed into a deep dark red, which was so not good. "Oh, hell, I thought it was over, and we could finally go on with our lives. But, I guess that's not in the cards right now," Eric growled as he took Jory in his arms and whispered sweet nothings in his ear. It helped because the alpha mate calmed down almost immediately.

"I'm afraid not, father," Chris softly said. Jory gently pushed Eric away, and the alpha let him because he knew that Jory had recovered, which was good. "We need to find the bastard who did that to you. If we find him, he will be punished appropriately," the alpha mate growled. "Agreed," said Eric and Chris simultaneously. "Alright," Jory said, looking at Chris. "Are you ready to meet with the rest? Because we need to inform them what's up and what awaits us," the alpha mate finished. Chris nodded; he was ready and would do what it took to catch the bastard, so the pack could finally pick up their lives again.

It was a given that everyone was glad that Chis was home again, safe and sound. However, many frowned when Chris told them what had happened during the aging process. And, of course, they all wanted to join the hunt for the bastard who had dared to touch Chris' mind. They all knew that someone's mind was private, and you didn't invade one's mind without asking permission.

The problem was where to start the search because no one knew who they were looking for. "We could start at the place where you, Carmen, Marcus, and Grace slept during the aging process," Dorian said. "To do that, we would need permission from Gaia herself," said Carmen.

Chris nodded; he would try to reach Gaia to ask her to give her permission to enter her world. "My sense of smell is very good, and I try if I can smell anything from the person we're looking for," Marcus offered. Marcus shared his soul with two spirits, a white tiger. After all, his mother was one, and a lion, because his father, Sheriff James Stanton, was a lion shifter. "Make sense," Chris said. They decided that with Gaia's blessing, The Four would start the investigation.

Jory, Eric, James, and especially Max didn't like that their children would go and face danger once again. She took her time, but finally, Gaia permitted them to enter her world. Chris, Marcus, Carmen, and Grace held hands then they vanished.

"They will be alright," Jory whispered, but he didn't even manage to convince himself entirely. What if the person waited there for them? What if it was a very powerful creature? "You think too hard. Have a little fate, baby," Eric said as he gently kissed Jory on the lips. The alpha mate sighed and knew that Eric was right, but that didn't make it any easier.

Chapter Thirty Four

"I know it sounds strange, but I can't remember ever being here," said Grace. Carmen eyed her for a second, then said that she, too, couldn't remember the place. Marcus agreed with Carmen and Grace because he, too, didn't remember. Only Chris stayed silent, which earned him curious looks from the other three.

"Do you remember?" a frowning Carmen questioned. "As a matter of fact, I do. And I find it odd that the three of you don't," Chris admitted. "We can talk about that later. But, first, we need to start the search," Marcus insisted. "I assume that you need to shift?" Chris said. Marcus nodded because, in his tiger form, his smell was excellent.

Just when Marcus was about to undress and get ready to shift, Chris stopped him. He held up his hand. "Shush," he whispered. Carmen's eyes widened as a sign that she had heard it too. Then Marcus and Grace nodded, letting Chris know they had heard it too.

The Four carefully moved toward where the sound was coming from. "There, behind the bushes," Chris whispered. They moved slowly toward some low bushes and came to an abrupt hold. "I'll be damned," Carmen whispered as she stopped Chris from approaching the small child.

For a moment, they were too stunned to react because no one had expected to find a small boy, and he was softly crying. "Please, don't hurt me. I didn't want to do it, but he forced me," the small child whispered, his voice broken. Carmen's eyes filled with tears as she saw the fear and desperation in the young child's eyes. It looked like he was afraid that they would kill him, but why?

Chris tried to get in contact with Gaia because it was her backyard, but Mother Earth didn't respond. Chris debated what he should do with the small boy. Grace knelt before the boy, but she didn't touch him. "I'm Grace, and this is Marcus, and Carmen, and the big guy is

Chris. I promise you we will not hurt you," Grace waited a second before continuing.

"Do you know where your parents are?" she gently inquired. The boy shook his head but still didn't make eye contact. However, the kid had stopped crying, and for that, Grace was grateful. "Do you know your name?" she softly asked. To her astonishment and joy, the boy looked up and whispered, "My name is Romeo."

"Why were you so afraid of us? Why would you think that we're here to hurt you?" Grace went on, but the boy had shut down. Somehow, Grace knew that he wouldn't answer anymore. She eyed Chris, silently asking what to do with the little boy.

Just when Chris was about to say something, the boy spoke. "I didn't want to do it. He made me." Even though the child didn't look older than five years, he had an amazing vocabulary. Carmen glanced at her brother, who nodded in silent agreement. Chris had spoken and acted like an adult when he was just a toddler. Could it be that this child was similar to them?

Chris knelt in front of Romeo; he gently smiled down at the boy. "Can you tell us what you mean by that? That you didn't want to do it, but someone forced you?" he said soothingly. The boy looked pleadingly at Grace; it was evident that he was terrified of Chris. Carmen didn't hesitate as she eyed Chris silently, asking him to get some distance between him and Romeo.

When Chris was far enough away from Romeo, the boy began to speak in a soft, barely audible voice. It was so strange to hear the toddler speak like an adult. Romeo didn't make eye contact as he started to explain. "I planted that seed into Chris' brain," he whispered.

Even though they were shocked, all four managed not to gasp so as not to upset the boy any further. Grace took her time before she continued, and she noticed that she was holding Romeo's hand, and the boy hadn't pulled back. "See," Grace said, waving her hand at Chris, Carmen, and Marcus; "they didn't hurt you. And, they will never hurt you." She paused, then added, "Who forced you to plant that seed into Chris' head."

"Zachariah," Romeo whispered. "If he finds me, he will hurt me," the boy whispered. Chris, who had kept his distance, said again in a soothing voice. "Zachariah can't hurt you anymore. I won't hurt you either; you have my word." Chris felt relief when the boy turned his head and looked up, straight into his eyes. "You are like me," he softly said. "I guess I am," Chris replied, smiling gently at the boy.

"Do you want to come with us? I don't think it's wise to stay here. At the ranch, you will have the protection of the pack, and you will be safe," Grace said; she didn't dare pressure the child because he was already skittish. "I can't," the child whispered as he began to cry again. It broke grace's heart to see the boy so terrified.

"Oh, sweetie, of course you can," she soothed. "No," the child whispered, "I'm stuck here because Zachariah ordered a warlock to curse me." To demonstrate what he meant, Romeo tried to stand, but he couldn't. It was like he was glued to the ground. Grace eyed Chris for guidance. "Shit, a curse, that's not my area of expertise," Chris said.

"We need Cassandra and Annabella," said Carmen. Chris said that he would get them and disappeared. Carmen and Marcus sat down, but they kept their distance from the boy. Grace gently started stroking a strain of blond curls out of the boy's face.

"It's getting dark, and the dark is bad," the boy suddenly whispered. Grace was taken aback by Romeo's words. "Why is the dark bad, sweetie?" she gently asked. "Because then he comes and hurts me," the boy wanted to move toward Grace, but the curse didn't let him. So, Grace, perceptive as always, moved toward the boy, so Romeo could at least lean into her. That's when it happened. The dark descended so fast, preventing them from seeing anything.

The voice that spoke made them all jump, it was eerie and scary, but nonetheless, they would defend Romeo against this unknown creature.

"The boy is mine. Zachariah promised me I could have him." The voice, who didn't have an ounce of humanity in it, said.

"Over my dead body," growled a familiar voice they all recognized. Chris had returned and with him two mighty witches. "Allegro!" Cassandra said, and she sounded so menacing that even Annabella frowned.

Cassandra had lifted the darkness, and now they saw a very handsome man standing beside Grace and Romeo. "I don't like to kill someone in front of a kid, but I will if you don't leave right now," Chris said in a threatening tone that left nothing to the imagination.

"Kill him because he's evil," Cassandra said. "Yeah, she's right because he wanted to take Romeo, and he's terrified of him," Grace said. Chris wanted to end the warlock's life, but he wanted to question him first.

As if someone had read Chris' mind, the warlock suddenly looked up, shielded his face with his hands, and screamed. The next moment he went up in smoke, then he was gone. "What the hell just happened?" Chris growled. "Someone very powerful took him and probably killed him by now," Cassandra explained. "Shit," Chris growled.

"Anyway, let's free this beautiful child from that ugly curse," Annabella cooed as she knelt beside the toddler and gently stroked his face. Romeo smiled and reached for her, stunning Grace.

Epilogue

Jory looked around the room where every pack member was present, as was Armand, who sat on the love seat, arm protectively around JJ. Finn, standing at the door opening, holding Sarah tightly. Felicia, with baby Caitlin in her arms, Rose and Alex next to her. Annabella, Cassandra, and Dacian stood by the window, talking enigmatically.

Eric and Jory had decided not to tell Felicia about her daughter being alive all these years. Alyssa had been rotten to the core, and now she was dead. So, why tell her? It would only cause her unnecessary pain. Chris had agreed wholeheartedly, and Hades had promised not to tell anyone. So, Felicia was happy, and one day she would meet the right man, and who knew would have children again.

Even though they had decided not to tell Felicia about Alyssa, Jory was determined to find out who had taken the little girl and let Felicia believe that her daughter had died.

Max and James sat opposite him, their adult son and daughter to their left and right side. Dorian, Mike, Devon, Billy, Jesse, and Jake sat at the huge table, talking and drinking beer. Dorian was dating another shifter, who had come to Willows Creek to start over. Eric was happy for his friend.

Chris, Marcus, Carmen, and Grace sat at a table in the far corner. It looked like they were in a serious conversation. Chris had confided in Jory and Eric that he felt lonely. However, Jory knew their son would be alright; he had seen it in a dream.

Jack, the jaguar shifter, had his son Beau with him. Ares had his arm around Emma, and even though Eric hadn't been thrilled to hear that they were in love, he now knew that the God of War loved his sister and would protect her with his life.

The alpha and his mate glanced where Romeo sat, playing with the dogs. Beau sat beside the fireplace, reading a book and watching Romeo with interest.

The toddler was an estimated five years old, and still, the child had been able to penetrate Chris' mind, which was hard to comprehend. However, the young boy had done so because Zachariah had threatened to torture him before slowly sucking the life out of him.

"He's so small, so young, and still he managed to penetrate Chris' mind. It's simply unbelievable. Aside from that, I'm so happy that we found him; now we have three kids," Jory whispered. Romeo turned and scrutinized Jory intently, smiled knowingly, and turned his attention to the dogs again. "I think he heard you," Eric chuckled. The alpha mate was sure of that, judging by how Romeo looked at him.

"Daddy? Sage is hungry. Can I give her a treat?" Romeo looked expectantly at Eric because he knew that Eric nearly always gave in. "Of course, sweetie," the alpha smiled warmly at the boy, they had accepted as their son.

Jory turned his head and saw the sadness in the alpha's eyes; he knew who the alpha was thinking of. His smile was rueful when he said, "He's here with us tonight. I know that he is." "How can you be so sure?" Eric questioned. "Let's say that I have some friends in high places. Our Ross is here, and he's smiling," Jory assured his mate.

"I love you so much. Somewhere along the way, I must have done something right that fate gifted me with you, my mate," Eric softly said. Jory smiled. "Damn right," he chuckled.

Jory and Eric hoped that with the demise of Zachariah and rescuing Romeo, the pack would be able to resume everyday life again. Eric, even though not a hundred percent active anymore, wanted the ranch to continue breeding horses again. He wanted to wake up in the morning, have breakfast with his mate, and then they would decide how to spend the day.

The alpha wanted to enjoy the little ones playing in the yard, sitting under the apple tree, and discussing unimportant things with his mate. "I guess everyone is sick and tired of constantly looking over their shoulders. I just want to live in peace," Eric sighed. Jory squeezed the alpha's shoulder. "And we will," he softly said.

"Annabella and Cassandra still weren't able to identify the one who took and probably killed the warlock who wanted Romeo?" "Nope, unfortunately, they haven't yet. But, they will find out eventually," Jory replied. *They have to*, he thought, but he didn't share that with Eric.

Eric and Jory sat in companionable silence for a long time; both lost in their own thoughts. "Everything is ready; we just need the two of you," said a smiling Emma. Eric and Jory stood and followed Emma, who was, as usual, in Ares' company. "Smells heavenly," Jory said as he sniffed the air. "It does indeed," Eric replied, then the alpha frowned. "Who is grilling?" he questioned. "Chris," Ares said, grinning. Eric growled something unintelligent, but then he smiled. "Well, he's the heir to the Wentworth Pack, so he better learn early how to grill a perfect steak," the alpha chuckled.

The barbecue was a success, and everyone had a good time. Chris had proven himself to be a master behind the grill, even though he didn't eat meat.

"Daddy?" Romeo sounded panicked. "What is it, sweetie pie?" Jory and Eric immediately went to the toddler. "He's coming," the boy whispered. Eric and Jory both frowned. "Who is coming?" the alpha mate asked as he lifted his son into his arms. Romeo didn't answer but began crying. Eric alerted the pack to prepare for an attack.

"No, I've had enough of all the violence and fighting. No more," Chris growled as he vanished. Eric and Jory eyed each other, wondering where their son was heading and what he was planning on doing. "I'll recon he went after the one who poses a threat," Jory said. Romeo had stopped crying, and his following words made the alpha frown. "Chris will protect us."

"Sweetie? Do you know where Chris went?" Jory knew it was a long shot but hell; he could at least try. As expected, the boy didn't answer; he even turned his face away from Jory. "Down, please," the child insisted. Jory obliged and put Romeo on the floor, and the boy immediately rushed to the dogs, where he sat down on the blanket.

"Should we worry?" Eric asked. "I don't think so; remember when Chris was Christopher?" Jory said. Eric nodded because he remembered it like it had happened yesterday. "I wish Chris had told us what he was planning," Jory said.

******

"Ah, I was expecting you," said Hades. Chris shook his head. "Were you the one who took the warlock before I could question and then kill him?" he said. The ruler of the underworld laughed as he replied, "I sure did. It was fun." "Did you kill him?" "I did." "Good."

Chris had followed the trail Hades had left while outside the ranch. Romeo had sensed danger, and that's why he had panicked. Before Chris knew it, he had entered the underworld, but this time because Hades had wanted him there.

Chris considered Hades for so long that the ruler of the underworld actually began to feel uncomfortable. Finally, Chris said, "Are you after Romeo? If so, why?" Hades shook his head because he wasn't interested in the child; he was interested in Chris, but no way in hell he would tell him that.

"Then why were you at the ranch?" Chris wanted answers because this was getting ridiculous. Why had the ruler of the underworld lured him to his lair? Hades wasn't gay, or was he? Well, anyway, Chris wasn't interested in anyone right now. Still, Hades was an attractive guy. "It's confusing, isn't it?" Hades softly said, and Chris couldn't do anything else than agree.

"I killed the warlock who was after the child, so he should be safe. And as for guiding you here. I wanted to let you know that the kid is safe and that I won't pose a threat because it wouldn't make sense. I rule the underworld, and as long as you don't try to dethrone me, we should be fine," Hades said with a strange expression.

Before Chris could respond, Hades said, "It's time for you to return." Chris shook his head as he landed in the living room. "Where did you go, and why are you smiling?" Jory questioned because Chris had run off again, without letting them know why and where to.

"Ah, that's private," he said as he walked over to where Romeo was sitting on the blanket with the dogs. "Hey, little guy. I just want to let you know that you're safe. No one will come after you anymore, okay?" Chris assured the boy. To everyone's astonishment, Romeo smiled and said, "I know."

Eric frowned as he turned to Jory. "Does that mean that it really is over? Are we safe and can resume our lives again?" the alpha mate's smile was blinding when he answered. "Yes, my love, we are, and we can."

The end.

About the Author

Well, there's not much to say because my life is pretty dull. I'm sixty-something, and I started my first book in 2012. However, it was published years later, in 2018.

Some people call me a late bloomer, and I guess I am. I married my wonderful hubby when I was thirty-three years. According to my mother, it took me too long to get married and settle down. However, I think that it was just the right time. I don't have kids. I have one dog who is my life.

If I'm not working on a story, I spend time with my dog. I'm a dreamer, always have been, always will be, and I still believe in true love and romance. I loved Italy from the first moment that I visited the country.

Other Works of Haley

Julian - Grapevines & Skyscrapers Book 1

Reunited - Grapevines & Skyscrapers Book 2

Weddingbells - & Skyscrapers Book 3

Jory's Destiny - The Wentworth Pack Book 1

Family Matters - The Wentworth Pack Book 2

Insanity - The Wentworth Pack Book 3

Children of the Gods - The Wentworth Pack Book 4

Clash of the Titans - The Wentworth Pack Book 5

Guardian Angels

Christmas Miracles - A Voice from Heaven

Serigala Valley

All or Nothing – Serigala Valley the Sequel

The Assassin and the Florist - Assassins Book 01 Part 1

Prelude to Murder - Assassins Book 01 Part 02

The Escapee- Assassins Book 02 Part 01

Cochico Village – The Panthera Hotel

Club Ghost Town

The Rightful Heir

Dream Master – I Am Cain

Rescues – Dutch and English Edition

Rescues 02 Emma a Journey to Happiness

Don't miss out!

Visit the website below and you can sign up to receive emails whenever Haley Langwood publishes a new book. There's no charge and no obligation.

https://books2read.com/r/B-A-LNQJB-ZMBFD

BOOKS2READ

Connecting independent readers to independent writers.